With hard-eyed realism and
Khan brilliantly gives voice to
for the theatre drives her int
Amina is beaten by her father
lent by her teacher. Just down the road, worlds away, the death of Boulter's mother is commemorated by his mates in an act of arson; Mickey and Patch become heroes in the twisted wreckage of a stolen car. In these twelve haunting stories about Asian girls and white boys, Rahila Khan writes about the tangle of violence and tenderness – expressed and hidden – in all their lives.

Rahila Khan was born in Coventry in 1950. She has also lived in Birmingham, Derby, Oxford, London, Peterborough and Brighton. In 1971 she married and now has two daughters. It was not until 1986 that she began writing. In the same year her first story, 'Pictures', was broadcast on BBC Radio 4's 'Morning Story' and since then five more stories have appeared on the programme. At present she is working on a novel which, like many of her short stories, concerns the lives of teenagers on the brink of the adult world.

Virago Upstarts is a new series of books for girls and young women. Upstarts are about love and romance, family and friends, work and school – and about new preoccupations – because in the last two decades the lives and expectations of girls have changed a lot. With fiction of all kinds – humour, mystery, love stories, science fiction, detective, thrillers – and nonfiction, this new series will show the funny, difficult, and exciting real lives and times of teenage girls in the 1980s. Lively, down-to-earth and entertaining, Virago's new list is an important new Upstart on the scene.

Down the Road, Worlds Away

Rahila Khan

Published by VIRAGO PRESS Limited 1987
41 William IV Street, London WC2N 4DB

British Library Cataloguing in Publication Data

Khan, Rahila
Down the road, worlds away.
(Virago upstarts).
I. Title
823'.914 [F] PZ7
ISBN 0-86068-932-8

Typeset by Florencetype Ltd of Kewstoke, Avon
Printed in Great Britain by Cox & Wyman Ltd
of Reading, Berkshire

For my parents

Contents

Preface

The history of our emotional lives is the story of our food. Some things stop us eating. If we are in love and about to meet the person, we can't eat. Although people on dates often go out to eat it's not unusual to be so nervous or excited that the food is a total waste of money. The same happens at a funeral; before the event, people say 'Oh, I couldn't eat a thing', and then afterwards they go back and have a huge meal, *when it's all over*.

Love, death, violence, fear; they all put us off our food in one way or another. Why? I think it's because they all tap into the same set of emotions. And I think we don't always know what we love, what we hate, what we're frightened of; and that's why we often fight the wrong things and the wrong people.

The people in my stories fall in love and get it wrong sometimes because they don't understand it. Some of them cuddle hate to them so long that it begins to feel like love. Sometimes they love so much that it tears them open and the only way they know how to get back together again is to hit out at something or someone.

The most damaging thing is when they hate themselves, and turn their violence on themselves, or on members of their family because they remind them of themselves. That brings a sort of death that you can carry around inside you for a long time.

I don't understand love, or death, or violence, or fear any more than the people in the stories do, but I like being with them while they are learning.

Some of the people in the stories may seem very unpleasant, but I like them all.

Rahila Khan, Brighton, 1987

Pictures

The teacher looked at Amina's painting. 'It's lovely dear. It's so nice I think your parents would like to see it. You can take yours home as a special treat.'

Amina was disappointed; she wanted her picture on the wall with all the others. It didn't look any better to her than theirs did. She knew it was better than the ones with smudged faces and arms and legs that didn't seem to belong to the body, but it wasn't as nice as the very pretty one with the blue dress for Mary, and the light shining around the Babyjesus's head. It was all a puzzle, but she was often puzzled.

'Shall I put it on the wall first, and take it home when they come down?'

The teacher frowned and thought for a while. 'Perhaps it'll get dusty and fade,' she decided. 'You want your mummy and daddy to see it at its best.'

Amina nodded, a sign of defeat rather than conviction and put the drying picture on her desk, ready to go into her bag at the end of the day. The white faces of twenty-four Marys looked down pityingly on the brown face of Amina's picture.

She put the picture on the table in the room at the back of the shop where she lived and smoothed out the creases. It made a cheerful display in the dingy room. In one corner the television was on: piled in corners were cardboard boxes of sweets and crisps, washing-up liquid and soap, tinned fruit and little bottles of spices. The stockroom of the shop was too small to hold all the different lines that her father needed to carry to make a profit from his long opening hours and local trade. Always there was a slight sense, not entirely in the nose, of food smells and cheap unguents. These combined, rather than counteracted one another, so that all Amina's clothes carried with them a suggestion of this room. She had never known why people drew away from her a little on buses and in lifts. It was not always through residual dislike of her colour, but often because she smelled. Piles of washing, waiting to be ironed, drew in the atmosphere of the room and made it her aura.

Amina set about tidying a little space for herself so that she could settle to wait for her mother. She wanted to ask where they could display the picture. She hoped it could go over the gas fire. The television glowed indiscreetly in the corner and captured her mind. She sank into her chair and became absorbed in the invaders from space, the petty quizzes, cartoon chases, and finally the military music which announced the news. Little of this made any impression on her memory or her beliefs.

Her mother came in the room for a rest before serving in the shop for another three hours till nine o' clock. She was a thin woman who had spread in the middle. Her legs showed the slim girl she had once been and her ankles seemed too fragile to support the fat belly that rested high above them. When she saw Amina, the tiredness fell from her face, and the impatience, layered on by dealing all day with customers, dropped away. A smile plucked at the corners of her mouth and she spread her arms. Amina popped out of her chair like a cork from a toy gun and landed in her mother's arms. There was an intimacy between them that came from the knowledge that there would be no more children after her. Amina was the daughter of her parents' middle age. Their family was thought to be long over when she announced her intention of joining it.

The sharp contours of the little girl's body made comfortable hollows in her mother's soft flesh. They stood for some seconds, holding one another. Amina wriggled to free herself.

'Look.'

Mrs Iqbal smiled and waited for her gift. Amina reached toward the picture. The smile went from her mother's face as quickly as the tiredness and irritation had faded a few moments earlier.

'What is this?'

She never snapped at Amina, but the tone of interrogation was unfamiliar enough to the girl to cause her some anxiety. She did not want to anger her mother.

'The teacher sent it home.'

'Why? Is it not for school? Is it not good?'

Amina was near to tears. 'It is very good. Teacher says it is too good to spoil on the wall at the school. She sent it for you.'

Mrs Iqbal struggled to keep the emotion from her voice. She took the picture and folded it, first in half, then quarters, each time with a swift and neat crease. Then, she tore it across. The pieces were pushed into a bin. Amina squealed as she saw the destruction of her beautiful picture; but her mother took her arm, pulled her slowly but firmly to her, and sank to a chair, settling the girl on her lap. She pulled Amina's head down so that it rested on her experienced bosom and talked quietly to her.

'Who is in this picture?' she murmured.

'Babyjesus and Mary.'

'Why do you draw them?'

'Soon it will be Christmas, when Babyjesus came to save us.'

Mrs Iqbal felt her head tighten inside, but her questions remained quiet.

'What is this story?'

Amina told her mother how the angel had spoken to Mary, of the journey to Bethlehem, the shepherds, the kings, the death of all the baby boys, and the miraculous escape to Egypt. She loved the story. She told her mother of the pictures they had drawn of Mary and Jesus, the frieze that they would paint, the little Christmas cards that they were going to bring home, and the play that all the parents would come to school to see.

When the story was over, Mrs Iqbal waited for a few moments until Amina was still and comfortable again. Then she explained. 'You must never let your father know this,' she said. 'We do not draw pictures, especially not the Prophet from Nazareth and his mother.'

Gently she explained that the Prophet Muhammad had forbidden the drawing of the Prophet from Nazareth and his mother, in case they should be worshipped. She told Amina what a good and holy man Jesus of Nazareth was and how his mother was a great and holy lady, but that, for Muslims, they should not be spoken of as they were in the school.

That evening, Mrs Iqbal told her husband that she could not work in the shop, that Amina needed her. It was not good for the girl to be alone every night with only the television. All evening mother and daughter sat happily drawing together. Mrs Iqbal brought in a new box of coloured pencils from the shop, ignoring her husband's grumbles about expense. She and Amina drew and traced many beautiful patterns on gleaming sheets of white paper: lovely patterns, swirls and angles, colours and whorls, they darted in and out like small animals chasing one another through complicated passageways. They followed slow, sensuous curves, like young lovers courting one another through the elaborate ritual of a rigid but harmonious society. But there were no people.

Mrs Iqbal took the Quran from its shelf. With unfeigned devotion, she gently turned its pages, showing Amina the subtle and gracious designs which illuminated the sacred text. As they sat and worked and talked together, the bond of intimacy reformed between them and when she kissed her mother goodnight Amina was relaxed and happy.

At school, Amina drew her Christmas card. The same patterns that her mother had taught her took the place of the crib, with the oxen and asses. No wise men or shepherds interrupted the lively and sinuous decoration of her pencils. Her teacher was bewildered.

'This is not right. You should be drawing the stable.'

Amina was courteous but firm in her answer. 'I do not draw stables. I draw patterns.'

The teacher fetched her a new sheet of card and folded it double. 'Here you are, dear. Do another of your nice drawings of Mary and Jesus.'

Amina was surprised. Why did the teacher not understand her explanation? 'I do not draw people.'

'Of course you do. You draw lovely people. Just because we didn't put your last picture on the wall doesn't mean you can't do well.'

'I know. The last picture was too good to put on the wall.'

The teacher blushed as she remembered the lie.

'But, I do not draw people.'

The teacher determined to make up for her mistake in rejecting the picture. 'Now look, Amina, that was a lovely picture, and I wish now I hadn't let you take it home. It means that we haven't been able to see your work on our walls.' She spoke in a bright and encouraging voice, that Amina had not heard her use before.

'Here is a nice new piece of card and here is a sheet of paper. Draw the same picture on both, dear, and paint it, then you can take the card home, and we'll put the picture on the wall.'

Mechanically, she bared her teeth in a smile and walked away before Amina could explain again that she did not draw people.

For the next hour, as she worked, the white faces of Mary and Jesus smiled down from the walls at her. Slowly the pictures took shape. The paper and card were filled with the forms from the myth. Amina enjoyed the work and she had a delicate touch. By the end of the day, she could sit back in her desk and see the completed pattern, the Christmas card with its animals and Holy Family and the picture for the wall, a traditional, if slightly dusky Madonna.

The teacher smiled in genuine pleasure when she saw the finished work. 'See, dear. You're very good.' For the first time, she really examined the picture, ignoring the disturbing colouring of the features. 'Very good,' she said. She pushed the card into Amina's hand and whisked away the patterned card and the picture.

'Home time.'

That night, Amina sat alone as usual in front of the television. Her mother and father worked together in the shop, taking time only to put her to bed. The street light outside filtered in through her thin curtains and picked out the little bunches of flowers that dotted the paper on her walls. Half a mile away, in school, a brown-faced Mary smiled unceasingly down at a bin in the corner of the room.

On the top of the bin was a folded piece of card with an accurate and lovingly-reproduced illumination from the Quran. Below Amina's bedroom, in the shop, Mr and Mrs Iqbal sold Christmas cards, men's magazines, fairy lights, and crackers. In the litter bin, fixed to the street light that forced light in through the curtains of the little girl's room, lay a card, skilfully and lovingly produced at school that day. Amina had kept it in her hand all the way home, looking at it sometimes and asking the face on it what she should do.

In the end she had dropped it into the bin before pushing open the door of the shop and hearing the jingle of the bell as she entered. Rain soaked the card. The paint ran down, and the stiffness relaxed into limp decay. The Mother of God cradled her son in her arms, in amongst the orange peelings and sweet wrappings.

Mum

I've always had a good laugh out of baldies. In our family the men don't lose their hair. Grandad's eighty-two, and he's got a full head of curly red hair, just like mine. It's not tight curls, like a perm, but soft, wavy carrot topping. When I was little they used to call me 'Carrot Top', but I didn't mind even then. I just used to laugh because I already knew the real joke was being bald. Dad's hair's different, thick, black and wiry. At least it was black, but it's started to go grey at the sides. Really good it looks, like he was a judge or someone important, not just a van driver. Not that there's anything wrong with being a van driver; that's what I'm going to do when I leave school. Dad can swing it with his boss, who's always taking people on who let him down. He knows Dad's reliable, so he'll give me a try. I'm learning already. Dad takes me out to an old airfield and lets me have a go round in the van. Dead easy. So, I should get through a test as soon as I'm old enough. Then I can do part-time relief with Dad until I've got a clean licence for a year; then I'll be on my own.

Dad's boss is a bit of a baldie, so I'll have to be careful. Dad calls him 'The Eagle' at home because he's bald and he's got this really hooked nose. When he's not happy, old Willey, Dad's boss, Dad says he stretches his neck and lets his head swing left and right just like an eagle looking for a corpse to swoop down on and have a rip at. Sort of pathetic because he's bald, but a bit dangerous too; won't exactly kill you himself, but he'll be glad enough to swallow the flesh when someone else has done the dirty work. Anyway, I can watch it while I'm around him and have a go at all the other baldies.

Mum loves our hair. She's always washing it for us. All of us, not just the little kids. It's great having your hair washed. Mum leans us over the basin in the bathroom and turns the shower hose onto us. She never lets it get too hot to scald you, but always tests it on herself first. Dad and Grandad squat by the basin and crick their backs; I think they only go through with it because Mum likes doing it. But me, I love her to do it. I get a stool and I put it with its back to the basin and I lean backwards so that the hair drops away from my face into the water. Mum stands up close and I look at her while she sprays the water over and works in the shampoo. It's better than a night's sleep at making you feel relaxed and ready for anything. We talk about things while she's massaging the lather in with her fingertips. I used to tell her about how I got at baldies, but of course, I don't anymore, even though I hate them more now than I did before, before it all happened. It was dead good, having your hair washed like that. Not like your mum, more like a friend.

I used to tell her about how we would hang out of the top window of the bus and see who could get the most baldies. I started it. No one else at school seemed to bother about them. They'd even given up calling me 'Carrot Top' when they could see I didn't mind it.

At first we used to take it in turns to call out to them. When it started you got a point if you just dared to shout 'Baldie' out of the window. But that was too easy because we all did it all the time. There didn't seem any point in not doing it. Then we made it so that you only got the point if the baldie looked round and waved his fist at you or shouted back. That was more fun, but Wallo stopped that. Wallo's a bit too clever, really. He said that, as we took it in turns to shout and as the person would react like he did whoever shouted at him, it was a game of chance, not a game of skill, a bit like tossing a coin or throwing dice. Wallo said that as we had no personal influence on the outcome, our successes were arbitrary – Wallo speaks like that, it'll get him into trouble one day. Anyway, what happened was, Wallo said we had to throw something at the baldies. We still took it in turns, but we had to hit them actually on the head to get the point.

Well, you'll realise this really was a bit of fun and needed a lot of skill, especially when the bus was moving, and if it wasn't moving you were a fool if you tried it because obviously the baldie could just jump on and there you were, trapped on the top deck of a bus with an angry baldie running up to get you.

After a bit we moved on to include wigs. In a way, they're even more funny than bald heads because a baldie obviously doesn't mind too much being bald, but if you wear a wig, you must feel really hurt about being bald because you've spent all that money covering it up. It's dead easy, spotting a wig, they always show. At least, I think they do. I suppose that there might be good ones that you don't know about because they're so good you can't tell.

We started like we did with the baldies, just shouting out 'Rug' or 'Syrup' (you know 'Syrup of Figs – wigs'), and pointing and jeering to make them angry. It nearly always worked which just proves my point, really, that they must mind a lot or they wouldn't be wearing the wig. Throwing things at them wasn't as good as with the baldies because the wig was protection: a good bald head shining up at you is a real invitation to hit it. So, we decided to think of something else. It was Wallo who came up with it. It always is Wallo who sorts things out; he's too clever for his own good, really.

I told Mum about the plan when she was washing my hair. Dead good it was, just the two of us in the steamy bathroom, her stroking away at my temples and humming a bit in this way she had when she was happy and me telling her about the next stage in the war on the baldies. Once or twice, I'd thought that she didn't like us doing it, but she never said and she always laughed at the really funny ones when people had gone so red in the face that the angry blush had gone right over the top of their bald heads. It's true. When you're bald you blush right to the back of your neck. Anyway, I loved telling her about things because she didn't seem like a grown-up. She was only eighteen when she had me, so she's dead young and understands. Dad's only a year older, but he's like an old man in his mind and never sees a joke. She didn't laugh at the new plan and I nearly gave it up in case I was going too far and would upset her; I wouldn't upset Mum for anything. But she said, no, no it was really great, but she just hadn't been feeling very well, tired a lot, and a bit of a pain. It was all right, but it had got her down a bit. She said she'd be all right in a couple of days, the doctor would give her a tonic; but the plan was great, she really wanted to know how it would go. So we went ahead. I knew it would cheer her up.

When you don't need to see a wig they're everywhere and then when you really need one for a plan you can't get near one. The plan needed a wig right up close to the bus. We rode around for weeks with all the equipment before we got a chance to try it out. All we used was a reel, some fishing twine and a hook. Every day, on the bus to school and home again, we scouted the streets for wigs. We'd often see one yards from the kerb so we always shouted, but there wasn't one beneath the bus window for ages.

At last we were lucky. Scab spotted him and I had a go because it was my fishing tackle. It was the riskiest so far, but it was the best because it was so dangerous. It was the closeness of the victim that gave it its extra attraction. When the bus pulled up at a stop, Scab noticed the man in the syrup. He was standing with his back to the bus, talking to an old woman. Scab grabbed my arm and pointed. Wallo grinned. It was perfect. It wasn't one of those old wigs, you know the ones; they were bought fifteen years ago, a perfect match with the ring of hair around the skull, but as time's gone on, the real hair's gone pepper-and-salt grey, while the wig's stayed black. You often see it. I suppose the bloke knows it doesn't look convincing any more, but he's not as proud as he was and, anyway, he's grown attached to it and doesn't think he can face going out one day without it and going bald all at once. All his friends know about it, but they're all too polite to say anything. Well, it wasn't one of those. It was new and it fitted a treat. Only a keen wig-spotter could have told. There was something about the colour that didn't quite work and it was very thick at the roots so that you couldn't see any scalp peering through anywhere, like you can with even the thickest head of real hair.

Well, I pulled the twine out and cast it down through the bus window and swept it about over his head. Wallo rang two sharp jabs on the bell and the driver pulled away. The hook bit, staggered a second trying to find purchase, and then the lurching of the bus dug it into the wig and as we pulled away the hair ripped off and dangled behind us. The man's hand flew to his head and the old woman gaped at him. We fell over in agonies of laughter. I managed to keep the wig out of sight while the conductor rushed up and shouted at us for starting the bus. He was going to kick us off but we were crying for the fun of it and we couldn't pay any attention to him. In the end, he didn't have the nerve to do anything, so he just grumbled a bit and went away.

I took the wig home to show Mum, but she wasn't there. The doctor had looked at her, pulled a face and sent her off to the hospital for tests.

It was a couple of months before she came out. They'd cut the pain out of her, but she still wasn't well. She had to keep going back for treatment. I washed my own hair after that. She couldn't bend to do it.

After a bit, with the treatment, her hair all fell out and her eyebrows. She wears a wig now, and she's not young anymore. It's a good wig, just like the one we plucked off the baldie's head.

I don't do wigs anymore. But I hate baldies more than ever. Wallo and Scab won't join in now. I don't throw things, I gob out of the bus windows all over their heads. I'm not as careful as I was either. One day, I gobbed on someone and he ran and got on the bus. Good runner he was. He flew up the stairs and came and pushed his face at me. He hadn't even bothered to wipe his head and a great gob of spit was sliding down it. He was really angry, and shouted at us, which one did it? I stood up and faced him. I'm not a kid anymore, and he just looked at me and then turned and got off. I think he knew that I was angry too. Serve them right. In our family the men don't lose their hair.

The Angel

'The angel,' she said. 'Tell me the one about the angel again.' And her mother smiled, hugged the little girl to her and wondered what it was in the story than entranced her. Amina listened with her eyes shut as her mother told her the old tale of the writing of the Quran, of how the Prophet, at prayer in a cave in the desert, was visited by the angel.

'"Recite," said the angel. "In the name of thy Lord, who created man from clots of blood."' As she told the story, the woman looked down at the curled body in her lap, and at the closed eyes in the brown face. It seemed such a fierce and hard story to tell a little one, she thought, and yet, Amina loved it.

In Amina's mind, behind the dark closed lids of her eyes, a picture rose up of a splendid, robed angel, arms outstretched, with golden tumbling hair and bright, blue eyes.

'I know the angel,' she whispered to her mother when the story ended. 'The angel is beautiful.'

'Do you see the angel?' her mother asked.

'Oh, yes,' said Amina. 'Every day.'

She kept her worries to herself that evening. But as she sat with her husband, her mind crept up to the stairs to the small seven-year-old body in the bed above her.

'He is late,' the woman said.

The kind, bearded face of her husband turned to her. 'Yes.'

'Late, again.'

'Yes.'

'Always now, always he is late.'

What was there to say? She certainly could not argue, the boy was indeed late, as he always was.

'Yes.' It was a helpless admission that she had no idea.

'Too late. Much too late. It must stop.'

'You have spoken to him,' she reminded her husband. 'And he takes no notice.'

'He must take notice. He must not ignore his father.'

'I know,' she agreed. 'You are right.'

And from that moment, the evening became a torture. At every step that came along the street close to their house her husband looked up, leaned his head to one side intently and looked at the clock. But she knew the tread instantly. She knew that none of these quick trippings or slow shufflings, or measured paces belonged to her son. And she knew, as her husband knew, that the footstep would not be his for another hour at least. When Umar missed his supper he did not come home before eleven o'clock.

Furtively she scanned the face of her husband. Grey flecked the sides of the once-black beard, and grey brushed his temples. The lines on his face were the scars of smiles, not scowls. The dry lips, moving slightly as he read silently, had spoken gentle words to her in their long marriage. She had not chosen him as her husband; older and wiser minds had done that, but she gave thanks that she had spent her life with him.

He closed the book and placed it carefully on its shelf, the slow movements disguising his anger. 'I shall lock the door,' he announced. 'This has to stop. I make it stop tonight.'

'Please,' she asked. 'Not tonight. I shall speak to him.'

'Again. You will speak to him again?'

'Yes.'

'And how many times will that be? How often do you speak to him about this?'

She gave no answer. None was needed.

'Cars. It is always cars.'

'But it is a job,' she insisted. 'A good job, and he works hard.'

'What is a job if you do not live well?'

'We do not know.'

'We know.' He paced up and down the small room. 'We know where he goes. We know how he smells when he comes in. We hear how he talks to us. We know.'

She nodded.

'It's not cars I mind. I am glad he works in a garage. Glad he has a skill. But he should be here, now.'

'He is young,' she argued, pained to be opposing this good man in the cause of another, a younger and less worthy one.

He waved an arm dismissively.

'Come,' she said. 'Enough. We will go to bed. I shall talk to him again tomorrow.'

She took his arm, and he moved towards her protectively.

'Amina sees an angel,' she said into his shirt as he held her.

'Angels?'

'No. I don't think so, just one angel.'

'Is this good?'

'I don't know.'

'It is good to live with the angels?'

'In stories, yes. But I think that she means she truly sees an angel.'

'So should we all. So should Umar.'

And they left the door unlocked as they climbed the stairs.

The next morning Umar had already climbed into his overalls and gone before his mother could speak to him.

'Yo be good, d'y'ear,' he had warned Amina, in a rich Yorkshire voice.

'Oh, yes. I am good.'

He dropped fifty pence onto the cover of her bed. 'Here y'are.'

'Thank you.' She gripped his neck with her thin arms while he kissed her, then he was gone.

On her way to school, she passed the dark cave where the Prophet had been visited by his angel, she smelled the strange, heavenly odours coming from the gloomy interior, quite unlike any other smell she knew, not of this world; and overhead, swinging slightly, was the lovely angel who had spoken so mysteriously and thrillingly of making man out of clots of blood.

'Please,' she asked the angel. 'Make us all happy and look after Umar.' The angel looked down compassionately on her.

That evening, Umar came home straight from work and ate with his family. Across the table, husband and wife looked shyly at each other. It must be done. Who was to do it?

'Come, Amina,' said her father when food was ended. 'I shall give you a bath.'

Umar winked at his sister. 'And read yo' a story,' he said. 'While our mum reads us one.'

The door closed behind them. 'Well?' he said.

'Why do you speak so, to us?' his mother asked.

'What?'

'So,' she said. 'Just like that. So sharp. So hard.'

'I'm only talking. That's all.'

'Yes, perhaps. Perhaps it is only talk. I should like it so.'

'Oh, come on.' He rose.

'Please. Sit a little longer. Let us talk together.'

With a ill face he sank back into his chair. 'Well?'

'Yes. I think you know.'

'Do I?'

'Yes. You know how we are. You know we cannot let you go on like this.'

'What's this, then?'

'This drinking.'

'Oh.'

'Yes. You knew what I was to say. We do not drink. It is forbidden. You are not to drink either.'

This time he did stand up. 'Well I'm glad you've said it. I only wish he,' and he flicked his head to gesture towards the ceiling, 'had said it. Instead of making you.'

'What difference?' she asked. What does it matter who says it? It is true.'

'But he should. If anyone does, it should be him.'

Upstairs, Amina told her father about her day at school, about the teachers and the other children. He soaped and flannelled her, listening to her chatter, but at the same time, keeping a guard on the noise of conversation down below. When the front door slammed he sighed.

'Will you tell me the story about the angel tonight?' she asked.

Smiling, he agreed.

On Saturday morning, Amina ran down the road to the shops to spend the fifty pence that Umar had given her. Many warnings had been pronounced before she was allowed to leave the house.

'Do not cross the road.'

'No.'

'There is no need to cross the road. The sweet shop is on this side. You do not need to go over.'

'No.'

'And do not talk to anyone.'

'I won't.'

'If anyone tries to talk to you, you are to run straight home. Do you understand?'

'Yes.' Amina danced in front of the door, trying to escape the litany of caution.

'And have you got a handkerchief?'

'Yes.'

Amina turned her face up for a kiss and fled as her mother still fired questions at her. Shaking her head at her own foolishness, the mother smiled and watched the thin legs carry Amina away.

The cave with the angel hovering over it was on the other side of the road, the side that Amina couldn't reach because it meant fording her way dangerously through the river of buses, and lorries, bicycles and fast cars. So she stood and looked at it over the roofs of the vehicles. In the slanting early summer sun, the angel glowed with thrilling life. It looked too kind to speak about such terrors as making man from clots of blood, but Amina knew that its compassion and power came from the same source.

Beneath the outspread wings gaped the entrance to the cave, with its strange smells and muffled noises. Amina could see the darkness through the door, but at this distance could not hear or smell anything.

As she stood, looking, Umar approached, dirty from work in his overalls. Amina screamed across the noisy traffic at him, but he could not hear. He measured his steps towards the entrance to the cave. Amina continued to yell, but still he made no turn of recognition. Desperately, she stepped from the pavement and ran towards him.

Fussing over the lunch preparations, Amina's mother refused to keep looking at the clock. Amina was a scatter-brain, she thought, a daydreamer. Often she dawdled by the shops, looking in the windows, reading the cards in the newsagent's, counting the buses. She shooed her fears away like geese, but they honked their warnings as they fled.

The busy road, the stranger with the bag of sweets. Where is she? Why is she so late?

At last, fearful and ashamed, she slipped out of the house and made her way down the road in the direction of Amina's thin, disappearing legs.

Beneath a brightly painted angel, swinging in the breeze, and the large letters saying 'The Angel', Amina stood sipping at a glass of lemonade. Through the door, into the mouth of the cave, Umar and his friends stood telling jokes, drinking, and playing darts.

Umar wandered away and out to his sister. 'Here.' He held out a packet of crisps.

'Ooh. Thank you.'

'You like this?'

She nodded, and grinned up at him.

He tilted his glass down and poured some of the beer into her lemonade.

'What's this?'

'Shandy. Try it.'

She sipped. Smiled.

'Good.'

A hand swung down and dashed the crisps to the floor. Another, flat-palmed, smacked her head. She was stunned and amazed. Umar juggled the glass away from her before it could smash to the ground.

'Home,' her mother shouted. 'Home. Home.' And she seized the thin arm, dragged her away.

'So wicked,' she shouted over her shoulder. 'So wicked.'

There was no lunch. Amina was pushed roughly into her bedroom and left to sob. Her father heard her through the door when he returned home. He silently asked his wife, who told him everything. His kindly face looked bruised as he took in the news.

'Enough,' he said at last. 'It is enough. Now this ends.'

When he returned from the Angel, Umar was unsteady on his feet. He had stayed longer and drunk deeper than usual because he did not look forward to the meeting with his mother.

'So,' his mother challenged him as he entered. 'So you come home like this?'

'So?' The defiance was unavoidable in response to her tone.

'Such a thing to do. Such a thing.'

'What thing?'

'To give a young girl drink. To stand her at the wall of such a place.'

Umar shrugged.

'Don't.' She snapped. 'Do not do that. It is not right. This is what the drinking does to you. This is why it is forbidden.'

Amina crept downstairs. She hoped to put an end to the noise, the arguing. It was all her fault. She would say she was sorry.

'Oh, please,' she begged her angel. 'Please make it all right.'

'Him!' Umar pointed at his father. 'What about him? Why does he say nothing?'

The father raised his head from where it had sunk onto his chest. He hated to bring up his eyes to meet his son, hated the sight of this drunkenness and disobedience. 'Very well.' He shouted, unable to keep his voice low in his distress. 'Very well. I tell you now, I tell you once and it is over. You will not do this thing again.'

The boy sneered at his father.

On the stairs, Amina paused. 'Oh, please,' she repeated. 'Oh, please.'

Then her brother spoke again. 'Yo say so,' he said. 'Yo. So weak you make your wife fight for you.'

'Oh, please,' she whispered. 'Please. Please.'

Her father's voice rose up. 'This angel,' he said, and Amina caught her breath. 'This angel has done this to you. Well, I will stop it.'

Out of Amina's sight he raised his hand to his son. There was a scuffle and a cry, then the door flew open and her brother pushed past Amina and out into the street.

'Oh, please,' she kept on saying, as she stole into the room. But on the floor, his wife cradling his head in her arms, lay her father, blinking dizzily, his shirt front red with his defeat. The angel had visited them and unmade him back into the clots of blood from which he had sprung.

Furnace

Mum died quickly in the end. You think it's going to be really bad, but it isn't: it really isn't. She lost all track of time, didn't know what was going on around her. Sometimes I'd go up to her room and talk, and it was still all there: she'd ask about how I was getting on at school, was Dad still teaching me to drive in the field, when would I get my licence, how was Grandad looking after things for us? All the everyday things, just like it all went on normally. But other times it was like she didn't know about anything. There were no questions, no thoughts about anything outside her bedroom. She'd lie there, holding my hand, smiling, sometimes giving a wriggle that you knew meant that it was hurting her but she didn't like to say anything. Every so often she would put her hand up, and then the sleeve would fall away and it made me want to cry when I saw how thin and old-looking her arm was, and I remembered how pretty she had been last year. She put her hand up and pushed it gently through my hair.

'Carrot Top.'

I would smile, but I didn't mean it. I know she liked to do it, but I couldn't stand it, not any more. It reminded me of the days when she had washed it for me, all warm and close, talking softly, like we were now, only everything had been all right then. She was well and I was at school.

'Carrot Top.' But it wasn't carrotty. It was just the same as hers. Like fire.

It was best when she could ask questions, because it meant she wasn't feeling too bad, but it made things difficult. I couldn't tell her I'd been suspended from school, could I? Not when she was ill like that.

I suppose it was my fault, but he was asking for it. He was tall, really thin, and had one of those Adam's apples that stick right out and go up and down when he's talking to you. We used to watch it all the way through the Physics lessons. It's funny, he'd be talking to you, telling you all about some useless theory or experiment and you'd watch him really closely, like you were interested and didn't want to miss a single word but all the time all you were looking at was his Adam's apple wobbling up and down. And then, sometimes, he would stop and swallow and it would disappear out of sight into his throat and drop back again. That really made us laugh. We used to keep a score of how many times it did that during the lesson. I suppose at first he must have thought we were his best pupils, the way we looked so closely at him, but he got a bit rattled when we never knew the answers to any questions he asked. We couldn't, because we didn't listen. All our attention was taken up with counting the number of times his Adam's apple disappeared.

'I don't understand you, Boulter,' he moaned. 'An intelligent boy like you, and all you do is sit making fun and wasting your time.'

And then he swallowed, and his Adam's apple disappeared, and I nearly wet myself trying not to laugh. So I never learned anything much from him, and he got pretty fed up with me. I wasn't the only one, but he seemed to blame me for all of them.

Then one day, he cracked. We were all counting how

many times his Adam's apple would be sucked away into his throat before the bell went, me and Wallo and Scab, we had got to nineteen. And then he suddenly lunged at us. He pushed through, grabbed me, and pulled me to my feet.

'Go on then, Boulter.'

'What?' I asked. I wouldn't call him 'sir'. I wouldn't call any of them 'sir'. Most of the time they didn't mind, but today it riled him.

'Sir, when you speak to me. So go on. Tell me what it what it was I just asked you.'

'You tell me,' I said.

For a second he stopped. His face screwed up like he was in pain. I was a bit frightened, but then, suddenly, he swallowed. His Adam's apple went straight out of sight, and Wallo whispered, 'Twenty.'

That did it. I spat out a great laugh, right in his face. Nearly blew him over. He held himself, tight, the way Mum does sometimes when she doesn't want you to know how much it hurts. Then he grabbed my hair. 'Stupid. Stupid. Red-haired lout.' And he shook me.

I really didn't think. And in a way I wish I hadn't done it. But I did, and I won't say sorry. I pulled my arm back and hit him straight in the throat. He staggered, clutched at his Adam's apple, and slid down to the floor. The rest of the class didn't move, didn't make a sound, and we could hear him gurgling.

'That's it,' said Wallo, very quietly, and Scab said, 'Better be off.' So I went.

I took my time going home. I didn't want to be early, though I knew Dad would find out about it sooner or later. I went along the railway embankment, between the lines and the cemetary. When we were little we used to go there and put tuppenny pieces on the tracks. They shot off as the trains went over them, and then we scrambled about in the stones looking for them. The more times a train went over them the thinner and more uneven they got until you could bend them in your fingers.

Trains didn't come all that often and we would have a laugh while we were waiting, looking at the cemetary. There were four men who dug the graves and we used to pick up the gravel from between the tracks and lob it at them. They shouted and swore at us, but they couldn't do much because they had to behave while the hearses came and went. And anyway, there was a steep bank dropping down to the graveyard fence and they would never have got up it. We'd have smattered them with rocks before they got halfway.

I tried a few coins that afternoon, but had no luck. I couldn't find any of them after the train had thrown them clear.

Mum was bad that night. I sat with her for a while, but she could hardly talk, so I just held her hand. Before the illness, before they cut the thing out of her and gave her the drugs that took her hair and eyebrows away, she had been so young, so easy to get on with. Whenever you were with her you felt like there was something happening. I have lots of laughs with my mates, but never as many as I used to have with Mum. When I was with her it was like standing round the fire on fireworks night. All around you it's dark and cold. You can feel the foggy night rubbing against your back and making you shiver, but in front of you the fire was red and glowing, scorching your face it was so hot. And in the darkness above and around, sudden bright explosions stunned your ears and your eyes, leaving an after-trail that dragged through your mind. Even after they'd finished you kept them in your head.

That's what it had been like. Now, she lay there, cold

and quiet. I told her jokes sometimes, sometimes I told her about the funny things that happened at school, but although she smiled there was no fire there any more. So I stopped trying to set it alight any more and I just sat with her and held her hand.

Dad was fed up when he found out I'd been suspended. 'As if we hadn't got enough to worry about, without this happening,' he complained. 'Don't let your mother know. Just get out, will you.'

'Get out?'

'Every morning. Go for a walk. Go to the library. But don't hang around here.'

'No, Dad.' I thought at first he was throwing me out.

'And don't get into any trouble. Just stay away so your mother doesn't know.'

He had been to school to talk about it to the headmaster. I didn't care. I'd had enough school anyway. He didn't tell me about the bruise. Wallo and Scab did though. 'All over his throat,' said Wallo, with a satisfied look. 'And he can hardly talk. You really fetched him a good one.'

'It's going yellow round the edges,' Scab reported a few days later.

We were on the embankment, after school. I waited for them there every day to see what the news was. It was nearly the end of term and it looked as though my suspension was going to last until I was supposed to leave. That suited me, I didn't want to go back. The four old grave diggers were gone now. A yellow earthmover scooped the soil out in neat trenches and shoved it noisily back in again when the family had disappeared. The men who worked it were young; they weren't the ones we had thrown gravel at.

It didn't seem right, that big machine ripping at the ground, engine noise grating over the claw, dragging at the dusty earth. It was hard work. The summer was hot and long. The ground was baked solid so that the clouds of dust blew up when the soil was broken. From our railway line we looked down the steep slope, choked with tall grass and spiky weeds dropping parched to the graveyard fence.

'Let's meet in the park tomorrow,' Scab suggested one day.

I knew why he said it but I shook my head. 'It's good here,' I said. 'I like to hear the trains.'

'Finc,' said Wallo. He seemed to know that I wanted to get to used to the place.

Scab shrugged, lit a cigarette, and threw the match down. It spluttered in the grass, flared up for a second and then died.

I went back to school for one week. I think they had to have me back so that I could leave. If I'd been suspended at the end of term I would still have been able to go back next term, so they stopped demanding an apology and let me back for the last week. That pleased Dad, but I wish I hadn't gone back.

I don't know, I always thought of winter when I thought of dying. Cold days, rain, heavy skies, hugging yourself to keep warm. But Mum died on a hot day. I got home from school and Dad was sitting in the kitchen. He pushed a cup of tea at me. 'She's gone.'

I nodded, took the tea.

'It was quick. At the end.'

The tea had a thin film over the surface where it had been waiting for me to drink it. I sucked it down in two gulps. I looked over the table at him.

'You and me, now,' he said.

I nodded again. His face twisted into what he started off as a grin, but it failed in the middle and crumpled. I went upstairs.

The bed was as she had left it when the men carried her away. I put my hand on it, but all the warmth of her was gone and it seemed colder than the rest of the room in the summer's heat.

Grandad made me go to look at her in her coffin. I didn't want to, but I didn't mind, so I went to please him. I knew she wouldn't be there and when I saw the pinched face and the poor wig that had never been her right colour I wondered where she was, who it was I was looking at. I put my hand on her forehead. Smooth and cold. A stranger.

The earth mover was still as the cars drew up to the grave. I took a good look at the men who worked it and made certain they were not the ones we'd thrown stones at. They tried not to, but they looked quite cheerful. The bunches of flowers and the wreaths balanced unsteadily on the lip of the grave. We were standing on some strips of astroturf hiding the raw soil around the hole. The priest picked his way professionally close to the edge and went through the words. Like the gravediggers, he didn't seem too fussed with what was going on. A train shuddered along the line up on the top of the ridge and I lifted my eyes to see it.

Two humps crouched on the embankment. As I looked, a puff of smoke broke free from them. Scab had lit up another cigarette. I was pleased Wallo and Scab had come, even at a distance. I wanted to wave but couldn't, it would have upset people.

Dad was crying softly, but I felt just like the priest and the gravediggers: I didn't know who we were burying, and I felt nothing. Mum had not gone anywhere, but she wasn't here either. It didn't make a lot of sense, but it didn't hurt either. It was all cold, empty.

Just then, a shuffling from the gravediggers caught my eye. One of them was pointing to the top of the ridge where

Wallo and Scab were watching. I followed the line of his finger with my eyes. A small, black wreath of smoke was growing and moving down the slope. Dark orange flames licked hungrily up into the summer afternoon. Within a few seconds the fire was in our noses, and soon we heard the crackling. Two figures dropped down the railway embankment and sped away out of sight. The undertaker's men slipped the coffin quickly into the grave, and the priest brought things to a hurried finish. The whole bank, summer-dried, flamed up in seconds, thc fire racing across it.

I looked at the coffin in the hole and then up to the blazing slope. Faces in a carriage window stared out at us. The flame and smoke, the crackling, caught my head and jerked it. I looked at the fire and smiled, then down at the coffin. For the first time, I knew she was in there, and my throat clenched. The fire hunted down the slope and right into me, and all the tears that spilled out still haven't put it out.

Seeing Me

The classroom was filled with a low, persistent buzz of voices; not the studious hum of a group of people working in unison, but the constant, troublesome distraction of bored teenagers filling the gaps between bells. Above the noise, the teacher tried to keep some sort of continuity of instruction, but with little success. The average age of the group of girls was fifteen years and three months; soon they would be released into a wider world of boredom and neglect, and other authorities would try to occupy them between giros. Soon their days would be measured out by the regular visits to the Job Centre and the corner cafes. Perhaps they would even look back on the classrooms as places of relative happiness and occupation, places of companionship in lassitude.

In the midst of this education, a few girls still tried to keep involved, tried to prolong their learning to the last minute. They allowed the teacher to believe that the anarchic hum of the majority was a diversion from his real achievement. He ignored the chattering groups scattered through the room and concentrated on the faces which did turn in his direction, hoping for contact.

The greater noise never threatened to become overwhelming. There was an unspoken agreement that if the small knots of young women would limit themselves to intimate conversation rather than loud protestations or revolt, then nothing would be done. To an inspector, pausing outside the door to listen, the lesson would seem to be a well-disciplined free discussion period. Alongside the tolerated digressions about boyfriends and dates, new hair-does and make-up, about the latest film or television heroes, and fantasies about jobs, alongside these, the teacher kept his little group entertained with expeditions into short stories, novels and plays. As an English lesson went, it was not unsuccessful. For one of the girls, it was the most important part of her day.

Amina was a lonely girl, and she had found more friends and companions in the books described in her English lessons than she had in the corridors and playgrounds of the school. It was not that she didn't fit into the school because of her colour – nearly half of the girls were Asian or Afro-Caribbean. She didn't fit because she was too English, not because she wasn't English enough.

By the time Amina was born, her brothers and sisters were nearly old enough to leave home. Kept in at home in the afternoons and evenings, she never had the opportunity to meet other children her own age. The little corner shop where she lived made overwhelming demands on her parents; it was open until nine o'clock every evening, including Sundays, so until quite recently she was already in bed by the time her parents were free. Her evenings were not spent in the quiet enclosed Urdu world of other girls, or in the lively chattering groups of teenagers on the streets. Alone, she would sit watching television programmes, or she would wander in her mind through the dirty streets of the London of Dickens, or the hot, inexorable country lanes of Thomas Hardy. Amina's view of providence and circumstance had a pessimistic nineteenth-century colour. The Yorkshire moors of the Brontës had more life and dramatic conviction for her than the drab Midlands streets outside the shop, with its vandal-proof grill, its sturdy bolts and shabby, mismatched displays of sweets, cleaning materials and magazines.

And the people: Amina recognised the people from the television programmes when she saw them in the street. There was no doubt they were of the same type. But she never met the people from the books. She hoped one day to go to London, so that she could see people like Mr Jaggers and Mr Jarndyce. She had never been to the country, so she didn't expected to meet the rough, strangely courteous people of the Hardy books, but she never doubted they were there.

It was in the English lessons that she was able to ask about the people in the books. The teacher was always ready to spend time answering her endless questions. Sometimes he hadn't read a book she would ask about, especially some of the ones by Dickens, and this surprised her. But he knew so many other books and stories that he was able to keep her moving all thc time to new people. He seemed to know all there was to know about life and about the people in it. Often he gave her his own books to take home. Once he had caused her to be beaten by her father.

He gave her a book by a man called Lawrence, telling her that Lawrence was a great writer who understood all about people. And so, because she trusted the teacher, and because he knew so much, she took the book home. It was called *Sons and Lovers*. She knew she would have to keep it hidden.

As she read the book, Amina felt herself growing in understanding. Her mind became clear for the first time. The people in the other books she had admired seemed to distort as she read until she saw them as grotesque parodies of living people. For the first time, she felt distant from them and, although this was only the beginning of an historical sense, at the time it was like a realisation of the absolute. At home, religion had been part of the atmosphere she had breathed, but it had never entered into her heart. This book was like an ecstasy of insight. It was a revelation. No longer would she look in the streets for people who could not exist, people who moved through a photograph of the past, slipping through the pages of books into the everyday life of a Pakistani girl isolated from both her family and those of her own age and experience. From now she would see real people and it was her teacher she must thank. It was the teacher who had understood first and then shown her.

But the book was first to break into the intimate stability of her family. She had taken every care to conceal it, with its suggestive title. When the book was out of her schoolbag she never put it down. She would read it in the bathroom or at night when all the family was in bed and she was safe from disturbance. The violence that followed its discovery was like the arrest of a prisoner in a reign of terror.

Her bedroom door was pushed open, slamming against the wall with the force of the entrant. Before she could turn, half-awake, Amina was grabbed by the arm and pulled up in bed. Losing her balance, she nearly slipped over the edge onto the floor. Her father caught her and held her in a rigid embrace, slightly away from him.

There was anger in the man's face, and surprise and fear in the girl's. The sudden shock from sleep left a sensuous and yielding mark on her features. Her hair was in wild disorder and she fought to pull the bedclothes up to her chin.

'Yes. Look.' Her father saw the direction of Amina's stare as her eyes focused after the jolt from sleep. 'Look. Such a book. In your bag.'

Amina was frightened, but she made no response to her father. Rather than causing his anger to abate, this silence seemed to increase it.

'You must answer,' he demanded.

'You have not asked me anything,' Amina replied in a steady voice.

Her father's hand rose to strike her, but he hit her only with more shrill words, not with any blow.

'Why do you read this? Where is it from? Who gives you such a book?'

The questions showered down and Amina made no attempt to answer any of them. At last the questions stopped and blows showered down in their place. Amina's mother tried to put herself between her husband and her daughter, but she was pushed away.

Through it all, Amina stayed silent. At last, it was over. The man left the room and the two women, one old and experienced in the brutality of life, the other young and fresh to its hurtful inequalities, stared after him. Amina's mother gathered the girl into her arms and rocked back and forth, crooning tunelessly.

There was no hiding the truth. Amina's father eventually discovered the owner of the book. He complained to the school, and threatened to take his daughter away for the few months that remained to her before the law said that she could leave.

A smooth and carefully worded letter from the headmistress poured wine and oil on his wounded pride. Amina would certainly not be allowed to borrow any books of which her father might disapprove and her reading would all be checked by the headmistress herself. Proper respect would be given to the religious and cultural standards of such a caring home.

Amina's father felt able to allow her back to school.

Amina was at first ashamed at the incident and she was afraid that the teacher would punish her in subtle and furtive ways. But nothing seemed altered. The life of the class went on as before. She still joined the small group of girls who paid attention while the others went their own ways. Slowly, she recovered her own pride and even grew to respect her teacher more. After all, he understood. He did not embarrass her with reference to the difficulty and he did not ask for the return of the damaged book. Within herself she held inviolate the insight she had gained from reading the book and the relationship with the one man who could teach her something about insight into other people and herself. At least there was one person who knew how she felt and who respected her.

She decided that although it would cause her great shame and would be difficult to express, somehow she would thank him. A few days before the end of term, when she would leave the school for ever, she lingered after lessons had finished to catch him alone in his classroom and to thank him, both for his teaching and for his discretion over the matter of the book.

When the noise of pupils banging down desk lids and shouting their goodbyes had died down, she made her way softly to his room to look in and see if there was a moment when he would be alone for her to speak. She made no sound as she drew near to the door. She didn't want to invent a lie if he wasn't alone.

A few minutes later, she sped back along the corridor, paying no heed to the slamming of her feet against the dusty floor or the shattered silence as the door swung shut after her.

That evening, she announced that things were still bad at school and that they expected her to read more bad books. She had learned her lesson she said, she did not want to be exposed any more to their dangerous teaching. Her father nodded agreement and asked no questions. The days remaining were few. By the time the school organised itself to object to her absence, term would be over and she would be free. He did not expect there would be any problem.

The next day Amina started work in the shop. For several nights she lay awake, tired from the day behind the counter, running over in her mind the conversation she had overheard as she had silently approached the classroom. Her teacher was speaking in a low voice, and she had strained to catch his words.

'Only a few days, thank God. What a hellish term.'

'Glad it's over?' his colleague had asked, with little real interest.

'Fifth form lessons are always a pain. Most of them never want to learn. D'you know, this year I nearly got the sack.' And he began the tale of Amina and the book. As he told it, the colleague's interest became genuine.

'Why did you do it?' the other teacher asked at last. 'These Paki girls never come to anything. It's a waste of time sticking your neck out.'

Her own teacher's face was hidden from Amina as she listened through the open door. She did not see the slight flinch he gave as the question was asked, almost as though a fist had been raised to strike him. There was a long pause before he answered.

'You're probably right. Strange though. I used to think . . .'

But Amina's footsteps beating through the corridor meant that the sentence hung unfinished between them.

Party Time

This teacher really took me by surprise. It's not often they do that. Usually you can tell exactly what a teacher is going to say. There's never anything new. It doesn't really matter who the teacher is. Some of them think they're kind; some like to think they're pretty hard, like to see themselves as tough: either way, it doesn't matter, they all say the same thing whatever you do. Some of them say it in a voice that tries to be gentle and understanding, the others just go straight in with the withering sarcasm, but it amounts to the same.

And one of the things is, they never talk to you about anything real, nothing personal. You know, you hit someone in the face, and they ask you how you would like it if someone bigger than you lobbed one on you. Stands to reason you'd hate it. Then they talk about justice, fair play, caring for others; what they never talk about is the sensible thing – why you hate the guy you hit. They seem frightened of that, like it might be important and difficult to talk about.

Then usually they sweep you off to the Head so that he can lay one on you because he's got more power on his side than you have, and you can't refuse to hold out your hand for the stick or touch your toes in front of him and a witness because if you do, he'll only do something more dangerous, and then you lose more than if you'd done as you were told. And they know that, and you know that, so you go along with it even though you know that you'll get your own back one day.

Anyway, the point is this, one day this new teacher, this Porter, asked me a real question. I couldn't believe it. He had only been in school a few weeks and we hadn't made up our minds whether we hated him or just didn't care either way and could ignore him. Me and Scab and Wallo – they're my best friends – tried him out a few times, acted up, answered back, the usual, just to see what he'd do; but he didn't really do anything. He didn't shout but he didn't ignore it either and we were a bit puzzled what to do next. Then one day he did something normal and I thought I'd got him. Scab had been kicking the chair in front of him, not vicious, just kicking a bit when the lad on it, Butler, turned round and gave him a mouthful.

'Keep your feet still.'

Scab looked a bit and then kicked again, harder.

'Do that again, and I'll rip your face off.'

Porter looked across, but before he could do anything, I thought I'd get my bit in. 'Go on then, Butler. Rip it off. Might make him look prettier.'

Well, of course, all the class laughed a lot, even Butler. Scab laughed as well, but he'd gone very red. I laughed with the others, but while they were looking at Scab and Butler to see what would happen there, I kept my eyes on Porter. I didn't think he would be too pleased.

'Stay behind, please,' he said looking at me. 'The rest of you get on.'

Well, I thought I'd won then. You always know that when you stay behind it's going to be the good talking-to. Teachers who can't face up to you properly try it on on their own. They're always soft, and you can get the better of them. I decided that Porter was one of the 'fair-play and justice' boys.

There was a bit of fooling when the bell went. Scab made a sound like a cane swishing as he went past me and Butler pushed me against the desk with a laugh, but I knew I would be all right. Three minutes of posh talk and then all over.

'Sit down, please,' Porter said, and came and sat opposite me. This was a bit off-putting. They either stand over you, or make you stand while they stretch out, but Porter looked level at me. 'Why do you call him Scab?' Well, I wanted to laugh again. 'Sorry?'

'You heard me, I think. Why do you call him Scab?'

I thought to myself – these people, they go off to universities and colleges, and then they come here to teach us something, and he has to ask me why I call Scab Scab.

'Have you looked at him?'

'Yes.'

'Well then.'

'Yes?'

'Can't you see?'

'His face?' asked Porter.

'Well?' I pushed myself up a bit, wishing that Porter had not put himself so close to me. Sitting opposite him with him looking like that was worse than if he had kept me standing up while he lounged at his big desk at the front. It was personal. He said nothing.

'Well. You've seen his face?' I repeated.

'Yes,' said Porter, 'I've seen his face. It's a mess. He isn't just carrying a bit of acne like the rest of you. It's more than that. Does he go to a clinic?'

'I don't know.'

Porter looked surprised. 'He's your friend, isn't he?'

'Yes.'

'And you don't know whether he goes to a clinic?'

'No.'

'You have a friend. That friend has a face which is pitted and scarred by a disfiguring illness. It is raw and scratched because he can't keep his hands away from it. As he scratches, it spreads and worsens. Puss and skin lodge beneath his fingernails. Red and caked with disease, that face introduces your friend to the world. And you, his friend, do not know whether he is being treated. Is that right?'

'Yes.'

'And you call him Scab? Never anything else?'

'Yes.'

'Then I repeat my question.' And he did. He asked me the first real question I've ever been asked by a teacher and I couldn't answer it.

'Why do you call him Scab?'

Wallo and Scab were waiting for me when I came out. They looked a question.

'Easy,' I said. 'Soft. Like all the rest.'

But I had a good look at Scab. I don't usually do this. Well, you don't, do you? I mean, once you've got to know someone, you don't need to look at them very closely, you know what they look like. So it was a bit of a shock to have a good close look at Scab.

Porter was right. He was a real, bloody mess. I'd forgotten how bad it was because I was used to it. But being new, Porter must have had a bit of a shock when he came into the room the first time and saw Scab. It was just like he'd said.

I didn't say anything to Scab. You can't, can you? Not just straight out like that. I didn't even like to look at him too closely in case he noticed.

The rest of us got spots and things from time to time.

Everyone does. It's a bit of a joke and dead easy to deal with. But Scab had looked like that ever since he'd come to the school when he was eleven. With Scab, it wasn't something that was going to go away very easily.

I didn't mind. None of us did. Scab was a friend, and his face didn't bother us. But I began to think about what it was like looking at the world from behind that red mask.

For a start there were girls. We didn't bother with girls a lot. Most weekends we liked to listen to records and sometimes have a bit to drink. Sometimes we could get into pubs, but usually they didn't believe we were eighteen because, of course, we're not. But we could always get bottles of beer or cider at the Off-Licence and we'd sit in someone's house and play music really loud and drink the stuff. We didn't bother with girls then. But if there were parties we tried to take someone. I've got a girl called Julie, sort of.

We met at a party. Johnnie Sharp was alone in his house one weekend when his parents went away, so he had a party. Wallo and Scab and I went together like we went everywhere together. There were lots of people and they were making a bit of mess like you do when you're drinking a lot. At first, Johnnie didn't seem to mind, then, when people opened cans of beer by shaking them so that it sprayed out on the walls he got a bit upset, but later I saw him opening one like that himself and laughing, so he must have got used to it.

There was dancing, so I asked Julie if she wanted to. I knew her from school. She was in the year below us. She danced well and we carried on for a lot of records until we got tired and I took her into the kitchen for a drink. Then they started some slow music, so we went back into the living room and danced again.

Wallo was dancing near to us with someone and he

grinned at me, but Scab had disappeared. I didn't think about it at the time, but I suppose he must have left early.

We weren't talking and so when Julie lifted her head up and looked at me with her lips open a bit it seemed all right to kiss her. She was nice and after that if I went to a party I always took Julie or arranged to meet her there. Sometimes we met on our own at the weekend, but usually, I spent it with Wallo and Scab. It was more fun. But after that first time, Scab never came to parties. We never asked him why not and we never pushed him to come. I think we always knew, but didn't want to think about it.

I began to think that I should do something for Scab. I liked being with Julie. It was good to press against someone warm and soft and to feel the wet of her mouth on yours. It made you feel really good and relaxed and very tight and excited at the same time. And Julie really could be fun as well. So I wished Scab could have a girl. I mentioned it to Julie and she said there was no point. 'I know he's your friend,' she said, 'but he's awful. I mean no one would want to kiss him with his face all like that.'

This was a bit of bad news. When you hear girls talking they're always saying things like, 'He's not really good-looking, but he's got a lot of personality,' or 'I know he's not great to look at, but he's very kind and gentle,' and here was Julie, saying that Scab's face was too bad for anyone to kiss him.

Julie's all right. I mean, she's got really good hair, long and straight and she looks good. She's slim without that horribly skinny look that some girls have. I don't really want to tell you what she looks like, it doesn't matter that much. I just like being with her. I can tell that other people think I'm lucky and I like that. And I like holding her. It's good. I can see that she wouldn't want to kiss Scab, but there are plenty of other girls who might. I mean, if you don't look too good yourself, it doesn't matter who you go out with.

'What about Shirley?' I asked. 'I've seen you hanging around with her in school.' Shirley wasn't what you'd exactly call fat, but she was too big to be good-looking, and no one ever went out with her. 'Can't you bring Shirley to the party next Saturday? I'll make Scab come and they can get together.'

I was really surprised at the way Julie took this. We don't argue. I don't suppose we see each other enough to fall out and when we do meet we're usually interested in other things than trying to get Scab a date. So it was funny when she disagreed with me. I didn't like it a lot. I mean, girls usually agree with what you suggest. That's one of the nice things about them.

'Shirley wouldn't go with Scab.'

'Why not?'

'Well, look at him,' she went on.

'That's the point,' I said. 'Look at Shirley.'

This really got Julie going. 'Shirley could have boy-friends. She doesn't bother, that's all.'

I didn't understand this. No one who could do better would go with Shirley. Scab was as good as anyone for her. I didn't push it though. I was beginning to get the idea that Julie didn't like being told what to do.

We spent the next few minutes not talking. It was good until she pushed my hand away and said: 'Not now.' She was still thinking about it.

'I'm sorry,' I said. And I was. I wanted to get my hand back inside her blouse. Scab was a good mate, but not worth all this trouble.

'I'll tell you what,' she offered.

'Yes?'

'You bring Scab to the party and I'll make sure Shirley's

there. Nothing else. If they want to get something going, that's all right, but no pushing.'

'That's fine,' I agreed. And it was. It really was. I like Julie.

Well, it was difficult to get Scab to go to the party. In the end, Wallo and I had to go round to his house and stand over him while he got changed.

I understood that night why Scab didn't bother with parties. Standing in the kitchen drinking while everyone else is dancing and things is really boring. Julie was there, dancing with Shirley. It's funny, I wouldn't want to dance with another boy, but even if you want to you can't. But it doesn't seem to matter with girls, they can do what they want.

With the lights all dim Shirley didn't look as bad as she did at school and in her good clothes she wasn't all lumpy.

I was having quite a lot to drink because I was so bored and Scab was pouring it down his throat. I think he just wanted to drink enough to forget that he was there at all. Looking at Julie dancing with Shirley, I wanted to go up and take over. I like dancing with her and I wanted to go up to one of the bedrooms afterwards. Not that Julie lets me go all the way. I'm not even sure that I want her to, but it's good to lie on a strange bed, holding on in the dark and hearing the noise of the music and the dancing and the talking and know that it can't get at you.

All the time I was thinking this Julie and Shirley were keeping their distance and moving in time to the music. Then the record stopped and they came through into the kitchen. I was really glad because this meant that I could load Scab off onto Shirley and start to enjoy myself with Julie.

I'd just poured two new drinks, and I held mine out for

Julie to take a drink from. She had one small gulp and gave it back, then she looked at Scab and said: 'Dance?'

But instead of pointing him at Shirley, she took his arm before he could refuse and led him into the room with the music. Now Scab has this terrible face, but his body is fine. He can run really fast, fight well, and in any game with a ball he's magic. From behind you'd think that he was going to be good-looking. It's only when he turns around and you see the raw-meat face that you flinch. So when he danced with Julie it was great. The two of them were striding and strutting opposite one another, pacing around like they were animals about to spring together and fight. I thought, this is all right, Shirley will dance with him when Julie's finished; she's really bright, Julie, not pushing them together.

So I looked at Shirley. 'You?'

'All right.' And we danced. Like I said, she was much better than she looked at school, but I still couldn't wait to get to Julie.

Almost as soon as we started the record stopped and a slow one came on. I was really pleased because I could change with Scab and hold Julie. I was beginning to think that it would be too late if we didn't get down to it soon. I moved a step away from Shirley, but Julie had lifted her arms, draped them around Scab's neck. She looked so lovely, her body open to him like that that I felt ill in my stomach. They swayed together to the music. Wallo floated past, holding a girl and dropped his mouth open at me, pretending how he was really amazed at what was happening, even though he knew that we were setting up Scab and Shirley. I grinned, not that I felt like smiling, shrugged my shoulders and reached out to Shirley.

Close to, Shirley felt nice. Perhaps all girls do. She was fuller than Julie, soft and rich. Holding Julie felt like being with another boy who was just made differently, she was slim and firm, but yielding. Shirley was like a woman, older and rounder, it didn't feel like she was fat after all, just that there was lot of her, but it was all worth having. Julie never wore perfume either, she just smelled nice and clean. But Shirley had this really heavy stuff on that seemed to mix with all the drink I'd had and make me a bit light-headed. I was going to be really glad when I finally got to Julie because I was feeling more hungry for her than ever.

I looked across to her and Scab and I saw her just as she was lifting her face to him, the way she had that first party with me, her lips very slightly open.

Well, Scab didn't need telling twice and his tongue darted between her teeth. I suppose you'll say it's easy for me to claim that I was really confused by the drink and by what Julie was doing and that I didn't know what was going on or what I was doing, but it's true.

Afterwards, Julie really shouted at me and said I should have known that she was only building Scab up, making him confident and making it look good for Shirley, but I don't know, it looked pretty real to me. How could you kiss Scab if you didn't want to? I think she was getting a real kick out of it, kissing Scab and snuggling up to him with me watching and all my mates who know she's mine.

Anyway, whatever the reason is, it happened this way. Shirley and I found an empty bedroom and she was fierce. Her eagerness took me by surprise. Julie is always so careful, so controlled. Shirley just raced at it.

Afterwards we didn't know what to say to one another. Shirley acted fine, like nothing had happened. But I don't know. I felt different. It wasn't that I didn't like her. In a way I liked her for the first time as I watched her putting her clothes back on. She just stood there, picking them up off the floor and putting them on, like we were both boys in the changing room. I didn't know where to look.

'Shall I see you again?' she asked.

'I don't know.'

'That's what I thought.'

When we got back down, Julie and Scab had gone. I went through the house, banging on all the locked doors, but they weren't there. It turned out that when Julie realised where I'd gone she ran out and Scab followed her. He took her home early.

Since then, Julie's told me we can go all the way if I like, but I don't want to now. Sometimes, in the dark upstairs at the parties, while I'm holding Julie and stroking her long legs and slim chest, I remember Shirley's soft body.

I saw Porter the other day. 'I know now,' I said.

'You know?' he raised his eyebrows.

'I know why we call him Scab.'

He looked really interested. 'Tell me?'

'Because we hate him.'

Bleeding Hearts

She had walked for hours when she finally saw the open door of the little church and went in. After the hot, dry dust of the street, the atmosphere was like a soothing drink. It was cool, aromatic, a mixture of polish and faint incense. Small coloured windows let polychromatic light play in patterns over the polished surfaces, but prevented bright glare. It may have been the slight fogging of the incense, but the space in the church seemed solid, as though it carried a presence which had to be pushed aside to make a passage, but which closed in after her and swirled and eddied protectively around. When her eyes had got used to the different light, she was able to make out the detail of the building. It was small and intimate. The seating was solid and gleamed darkly. Around the walls were little tablets with pictures of a man being tortured and killed by being nailed to a cross; a sort of lapidary comic-strip. Where the seating ended, there was a series of steps going from level to level, ending in three short steps taking you to an altar. All around the walls were statues. Her eyes, trained by the austerity of Islamic art, were frightened that the Holy should be made into such a cheap beauty.

There was one of a man in flowing robes: he wore a pointed hat and carried a model of a church in his arms like a baby. Another was even more grotesque: a bearded man reached out with both arms in frightful invitation to grasp her to an open, bleeding heart in the middle of his chest. He smiled in a tricky, simpering way: she hurried from him.

The biggest statue was one of Mary with Babyjesus in her arms. She was just like the pictures they had drawn at school at Christmas time, the one her mother had been so angry about. In front of the Mary statue was a little rack with candles burning in it. The light from it made the hem of the long, blue dress glow. She gazed up beyond the candlelight to her gentle, passive face. The statue stared back down, her eyes seeming to rest both on the baby in her arms and on the girl.

She sat for a long time watching her, thinking how fine it must be to be a Christian. She had always loved the stories of Jesus, of how he cared for people and how he loved his mother. Women are important here, she thought. Mary is respected and listened to.

The atmosphere in the church moved her and slowly she began to cry. She made no noise, but tears trickled down her cheeks. After all those years of being bullied by men she had finally found a place where a woman would care for her. She had been right to leave home, she thought, although as she looked back on the day it took her breath away. She did not know how she had dared to do it.

With no preparation at all she had quietly taken fifty pounds from her father's till when the shop was empty, and then, smiling a goodbye to him she had walked out. It was all so calm, so natural, that he had thought she was going down the road for a few minutes. By the time he began to miss her she was in a coach on the motorway, leaving the grimy Midlands town behind her.

She hoped that her mother was not paying the price of her disappearance. She had deliberately left when her father was in the shop, saying her goodbye to him so that he was the last person to see her; he was to blame for not stopping her. But that was no guarantee that her mother would not be called upon to bear the blame. At the thought of her mother she stared again at the face of the statue.

She wanted to pray, but didn't know what to say. She had been taught a Christian prayer at school, but it began 'Our Father', and she didn't want to say that, so she just carried on looking at Mary and hoping that she would understand.

She didn't know how long she sat there before someone came in and started to walk around. She paid no attention, but kept her eyes fixed on the face of the statue. She was so tired and hungry. It was early evening now, many hours since she had stood in the cubicle in the bus station lavatory and put on the clothes from the carrier bag, screwing up her old clothes and leaving them behind her, like a skin that no longer fitted her, sloughed off. The light trickling through the coloured windows was fading. Some of the candles in front of the statue had guttered out and the light from the others cast a mysterious halo around the feet of Mary. The bare toes peeped out from under the blue robe.

She sensed that the other person in the church wanted her to look up, but she paid no attention. She would wait until it was empty and she would lie on the bench and go to sleep. Food did not matter as much as the tiredness of the long day, the journey and the fearful, aimless walk around the harsh streets.

Footsteps made their way in her direction.

'Hello.'

She ignored the man.

'Hello. I'm sorry to bother you.'

It was dangerous to speak to the stranger. But a church should be safe.

'Please. I want to be with the Mary statue.'

'Oh,' the man replied. 'Oh, yes. I'm sorry. I'm sorry to break in on you, but we have to lock the church now.'

She looked at him for the first time. It had not occurred to her that she might not be allowed to stay in the church, that she might be forced back out onto the pavement.

'Please. I would like to stay.'

He seemed uncomfortable. His face was pleasant, warm and friendly, but he wanted to be rid of her. Like a Muslim, he was dressed in a long, flowing robe. It was black and had a row of tiny buttons down the front. One hand fiddled with a button, and the other ran through his hair, sweeping it backwards. His feet kept him on the move, as though he was walking away from her all the time he stood still.

'You don't understand. We lock the church every night. We need to stop people coming in to damage it.' His explanation gave a sense of firmness and authority to his apology for being so inhospitable.

Still, for all his firmness, he was treating her with courtesy, and that was a new experience for her. She stuck to her position. After all there was nowhere else for her to go.

'Please,' she repeated. 'I have nowhere to go. I should like to stay. I will not damage anything.'

This seemed to cause him even more discomfort, but it brought an end to his wandering about. He sat down on the bench next to her.

'You must have somewhere. Where do you come from?'

She turned away from him and stared at the face of Mary. There was a long silence.

'Look. I don't want to pry. But if you say you've nowhere to go, I need to know something. I can't leave you here, and I can't really throw you out. How old are you?'

She didn't mind this question. 'Sixteen.'

'And do your parents live near here?'

'My parents are dead,' she answered truthfully. No one was more dead to her than they were.

'But there must be someone, some family and friends?'

'I arrived today from a long way off. I have nowhere to go. This church will be enough for me for tonight.'

'No, really.' He became firm again. 'You are not to stay here. That's out of the question.'

She stared at him in anger and disbelief. 'But this is a church. All can stay here. It is in your Bible.'

'That's not quite true,' he said quietly.

'Then why? Did not Jesus accept all the people, the women and the foreigners?'

'Well, you say "your Bible", but you seem to know well enough what's in it. Yes, he did I suppose.'

'Then I will stay here, please.'

'Not here. You can't. It isn't safe. I'm certainly not going to leave the church open with you in it, and there's absolutely no question of my locking you in all night.'

Still she looked at the face of Mary. She would help. The tiredness in her body convinced her that she could not leave and she guessed that he was not one who would push her out as her father would have done.

Silence followed. She sat there with no sign of moving or helping him. When there is nothing to lose a person is very strong.

'When did you last eat?' he asked.

Still the girl looked up at the statue.

'I really would like to help you,' he persisted. 'But I can't do anything if you won't talk to me.'

The light continued to grow dim. Now it was only the candles that broke the gloom, and these were going out.

The priest reached forward, took a handful and lit them from the spluttering stubs in the rack. He pushed them down into sockets. The girl watched intently, as the light bloomed out from this fresh garland of wax.

'Why do you do this?' she asked.

'Well, to make more light at the moment, but normally it's to help to say a prayer.' Secretly, he had prayed with all the new candles that something would arrive to get him out of this difficulty.

'You pray to Mary?'

'You seem to know a lot about what goes on in here.'

'We learn at school,' she said. 'All the lovely stories.'

'Is that why you're here? You like the stories?'

The girl flashed a hard look at him, to make sure that he was not mocking her, but his face was earnest.

'Yes. I like the stories, but I do not understand your churches. They do not tell us about those in school. Only your Bible.'

'I suppose,' he said sadly, 'that if you know the Bible stories you know more about it than most English kids these days.'

She ignored him. 'You are the holy man?' she asked.

'Not exactly holy,' he said. 'Just the priest. We're not really expected to be holy.'

She kept her eyes on the statue as she drove her argument on. 'You have prayers to Mary and you are the priest. I love the stories and I love these people.' She indicated the statues. 'We have the Prophet. We have our fathers.' A shudder went through her. 'And we have our brothers and uncles and one day we have our husbands.'

The man sat quite still now, and silent.

'Yesterday, I am told. Here is your husband. I do not know him. I do not want him. I do not want any husband yet. So I have left them all, and now I am here.' Still she avoided his eyes. 'So, please. I should like to stay a little while. And I should like to talk to the holy woman.'

The priest looked around, then looked up at the statue.

'The holy woman? This is not a person, this is a statue.'

'No,' she snapped, angry to be misunderstood. 'I am not a fool. I know what this is. I should like to speak to a woman. A priest.'

'But I am the priest,' he said gently.

'But you are the man. I have gone away from men. Here is where men and women are equal. Here is where one man has one wife. Here is where God has a mother who is loved and respected. I have come,' she said, suddenly realising what it was that she wanted, 'I have come to talk to a God who chooses everybody and listens to all of us. Please, I should like to talk with a woman.'

'I'm very sorry,' he said. 'But we just don't have priests who are women. It has to be me.'

'This is true?'

'Yes.'

For a long, silent moment she sat, looking up at the face of the statue. Then she leaned forward, picked up a candle and lit it, as the priest had done, from the stub of another. She screwed it into place, flakes of wax stripping off it as it was made secure. She stood up.

'Thank you,' she said. 'I will go now.'

'But where?'

She shrugged. All tiredness had left her, she knew what she was going to, if not where.

'I am going to find a god for women.'

She turned and left the man under the figure of Mary, yellow light casting a flickering glow on his face. The man with the tricky smile stretched out his arms to her, but she rejected him. She didn't need his bleeding heart.

Dog Fight

Have you ever really looked at a dog or thought about people who have them in their houses? I mean, it's a really funny thing, isn't it, when you think about it? I mean, look at it. There's this animal, just like a pig or a rat, only you let it eat in your kitchen, sleep in your living room, slobber and scratch whenever it wants to. Don't get me wrong, I'm not against dogs, I like them. I just think it's really funny what people let them do, just because they're dogs. Especially when you wouldn't think they were that sort of person.

For instance, the Headmistress at my Junior School had a dog that used to sit in her office with her. Now she was a woman who hated mess. I think that she probably hated children, she never taught any, she just used to let you come in to see her if you'd been specially naughty. And if your nose was running or you weren't very clean or something, she didn't care what she said to hurt you. It was like she thought that the school was something she'd been asked to keep clean and the children had been put in there to make it more difficult for her, as a sort of test. I mean, you could tell what she thought about mess and children because if you had been specially naughty, and you were sent to see her for a telling off and a punishment, then she would make you walk around the school at playtime, picking up litter.

But she had this dog. All right, it was only little, not like a great big invading foreigner coming into people-world, but it was still a dog and must have done all the things that big dogs do. It scratched and licked and it had a bit of rug that it slept on in her room and the rug was all covered in hairs and it smelled sweaty with that dog-sweat smell that they all have whether they're like little rats or great ponies. Some of the kids used to say that if they got the chance they would kick the dog to get back at her for being such a cow to them, but I don't like that. Like I said, I like dogs, and I don't think it's fair to hurt her dog just because she's nasty.

It was Wallo who got me thinking about dogs. Wallo knows lots of things that you wouldn't think anyone would know. I think he must watch a lot of television. Once, Wallo sent us all Jewish New Year cards. He's not Jewish, but he'd seen them in a shop, so he bought some and sent them to us. 'Seemed a good idea,' he explained. But I don't think it was. That's another funny thing, people having the new year on different days. It doesn't make sense when you think about it.

'Want to see a dog fight?' Wallo asked one day. We'd been messing about a lot at school and getting into trouble, and we'd been breaking a lot of things, too, so we weren't very popular. Some people, when that happens, they try to put it right, do better and make up for it, but I don't know, it seemed a lot of trouble to go to and I wasn't sure they wanted us to put it right anyway. It felt a lot to me like they were as sick of us as we were of them. We were counting the days till we could leave school, but the teachers had this empty look that made me think they were looking forward to it as much as we were. I don't know why. I mean, when we left that would be the end of it for us, no more teachers. But for them, well, if you think about it, there was going to be another load coming up every year, wasn't there? Anyway, getting into trouble a lot meant that we weren't bothered what we did in a way. There didn't seem to be anything to lose.

'What do you mean, a dog fight?' I asked.

'Yeah,' said Scab. 'A dog fight?'

Scab's all right, but he's not very quick.

'A real fight. Betting.' Wallo was very cool about it.

Scab pointed to a dog in the street. We were leaning on the wall behind the school, having a cigarette. 'I bet you I can kick that one's head in,' he said.

'No.' Wallo was annoyed. 'Don't be a prat.'

Scab stood up from the wall, but I pushed him back. We never fight each other and I didn't want to waste time watching Scab pretend to offer Wallo out.

'Go on,' I asked. 'I'm interested.'

'It's my brother,' said Wallo, and I should have known then that we were in for proper trouble. Wallo's brother's been in prison for hitting people and he's not good to know. But we were really fed up, so we were ready to do anything.

'He takes the money at the door,' Wallo went on, 'and he keeps lookout during the fight. He can get us in for nothing.'

'All right,' I said. 'I'm in. What about you, Scab?'

Scab picked up a stone, threw it at the dog and nodded.

'Missed,' said Wallo.

Well, the place where the fight was was terrible to get to. It was in an old barn and we had to be there early so that Billy, Wallo's brother, could let us in without anyone seeing. Then we had to hide in a corner until the place began to get full. Once there were a lot of people there no one would know whether we had paid or not.

So it was only just about still light when we tramped up the track to the field that the barn was in, the clouds bringing evening in early. The slant of light through the door stretched out like a coffin on the muddy ground in front of the barn.

Billy looked meaner than ever as he met us. 'Get in and go over there.' He pointed to a dark area. We moved off.

'Glad you're out, Billy?' Scab asked, but we pulled him quickly after us. 'What's the matter?' he demanded, when Billy had stepped through the door and out into the dark.

'I don't think Billy's too keen to talk about prison,' I explained. 'Especially as he'll be back inside if he gets caught doing this.'

'Oh,' said Scab.

You wouldn't believe the place we were in. There was a sort of barrier made up of old doors laid on their sides. This was square, and there were old seats all around it. I didn't like the look of it, and was beginning to wish I hadn't come. Billy came back in, stepped into the fighting area and loosened sawdust out of a bag onto the floor. The doors were all different colours, picked up anywhere, I suppose, from tips and skips and brought here. But the colours weren't clear. It wasn't that they were dirty, you'd expect that, but they looked as if they were made of marble or something, all swirly and streaked.

Voices outside let us know that there were more people arriving. Then cigarette smoke and sweat began to fill the barn; loud laughs, a bit unreal, the way you laugh on your way to trouble, not happy, but determined to be noisy and cheerful. There were a lot of people and once we knew it was safe to step out of the shadows we had a hard job getting near enough to the barrier to see, but we pushed and jiggled though until we were on the front, able to hang over if we wanted.

There seemed to be a lot of betting going on and over the other side of the fighting ring from me I could see two big men standing over another man with tattoos. After a bit, he gave them a handful of notes and they smiled and went, but he didn't seem at all happy.

'This is really good,' Scab was saying to Wallo. 'When does it start?' Wallo didn't know. 'I hope it's a real fight,' Scab went on. 'Someone told me they don't let them really go for one another.'

'Is that right?' asked Wallo, like he knew something, but wasn't letting on.

The smell really was terrible, hanging in the air like a corpse dangling from a rope. Above the chatter and murmur of the men, almost like a tune in the background, I could hear the growling of dogs like pebbles being thrown up the beach by a frightened sea and I wondered where they were and when we would see them.

I saw a struggling. From the side opposite the door, a black dog was dropped into the ring. Sawdust sprayed out under its paws. Then it stood rigid. A thick hood of sacking covered its head and sneaking out from underneath a thick, bright chain writhed up the side of the barrier. The noise stopped and we all looked at the dog.

'Great,' said Scab. 'This is where it starts.'

'Got it?' said the man.

The chain was grabbed, clinked fast to another choker. A second dog, brindle, fell over the side. The chain pulled tight between their necks, the dogs unable to move more than a yard from each other. This second too was blinded with a coarse hood. Money moved from the men's hands.

'Ten on the brindle. Evens.'

The black seemed more used to the feel of the place and sensed the brindle first. It bent its back legs and squeezed out onto the sawdust, clearing its guts before the fight.

Hands reached over to pull the strings at the necks of the sacks.

'Ready?'

'Yes.' Then he swore as the brindle twisted away. 'No.'

'Yes?'

'Yes.'

The strings were slipped; the hoods plucked off.

A deep roar rose from the throats of the men round the ring, like they were the dogs.

The black was on the brindle before their eyes had got used to the light. It had jagged ears that made it look like it had done this before. There were patches of bare skin where old wounds had healed over. It knew to move, thrust in, frighten the other dog while it was still surprised. The brindle couldn't have done this before. The great black Staffordshire mouth locked in, its teeth nearly meeting through the brindle skin.

The attack hadn't really worked, though. The black had drawn first blood, but only from the side of the brindle. Pulling away, the brindle ran to the other side of the ring, but the chain pulled taut, choking them both and dragging the black quickly after him. The black lunged as it arrived at the brindle, sawed the air with its teeth, but slipped on its own mess and cracked its side against a yellow door. The brindle was learning the rules. It leaped on the black as it struggled, drove its body hard against it, knocking it off-balance. Then it nailed its wicked teeth into the black neck. A scream of pain shafted from the black, but it twisted underneath the other, rolling over onto its back, pretending to submit, dragging the brindle's jaws away from its neck, giving the opening for its own teeth to find the throat. The jaws snapped at the soft part underneath the brindle's neck. A little sigh came from the crowd.

The black was really getting on top of the brindle when a

spout of green vomit spewed onto it from over the barrier. It stung the black dog's eyes and his grip gave way. The brindle made a backwards burrowing motion and was clear. I turned and saw the sick dribbling down Scab's white face. Wallo heaved him up and dragged him out, but I couldn't take my eyes off the fight.

The brindle and the black scrambled to their feet and stood, shuddering: paws wide, spit bubbling out of black lips, teeth nakedly jagged, eyes fixed.

'Go on.' I looked up at the man's face as he shouted to the dogs, and all I could see in his eyes was his money.

The brindle snarled round to face the shouting. The black leapt and was on the brindle's throat again, shaking and ripping. Blood from the gash dripped down with the saliva.

The crowd yelled out at the dogs. The tattooed man was shouting loud. 'Go on. Go on. Go on,' he sang to the black dog. 'Go on. Go on.'

The brindle had stopped wriggling and fixed its feet square on the sawdust. The black was worrying at its neck in a squirming and squealing, its mouth painted with blood and spit. I knew now why the doors had that strange marbled look. The fight looked all over.

'Good lad,' shouted the tattooed man, satisfied.

Then, like it was asleep, the brindle dropped its head, nostrils reached down to the floor, little puffs of sawdust rising from the hot breath. It tucked its head down between the firm front paws. The black knew he'd won and shook harder; it grew wilder.

It pounced on the back of the brindle and it overturned on the round of the shoulders. In a wild acrobatic turn it rolled right over the top of the brindle, snapping its head back as it fell. The brindle, breathing regular after its being quiet so long, seized the black's face and in a single swing of its head ripped the side of the black dog's head away. The black let out a terrible shriek and darted back; but the chain had twisted round its legs, bringing it screwing back to the floor. The brindle tugged and gobbled at the loose fold of skin, dragging it further off the flesh. The crowd loved it.

The two men with the chain finally dragged the brindle off the black. The brindle staggered quietly away, looking ashamed.

I slipped out and watched them carry the black out into the muddy track. Then I went and found Wallo where he was standing over Scab. Scab had sunk to the floor and hidden his head in his hands.

'He'll be all right,' said Wallo.

'Did you know it would be like this?' I asked.

'Sort of.'

'Do you like it?'

'No. Do you?'

I shook my head.

'I knew I wouldn't,' he went on. 'But you have to look, don't you?'

'I suppose,' I agreed.

Scab struggled to his feet and lurched off. We followed him, steering him in the right direction to get him home.

Behind us, in the night, there was the sound of a shotgun.

'There goes the black,' said Wallo.

Daughters of the Prophet

Always the men. Always the father. At little school, the headmaster made us say a prayer called the 'Ourfather'. I did not like to, not to a father. My thoughts were not for a father. It frightened me to think that a father could see into my head, so I moved my lips over and over again, saying the next word: 'Wishart'. I did not understand it. Was it the name of the father? 'Ourfather, Wishart in Heaven'. It made no sense, but I tried not to let it hurt me. Only men hurt me: fathers, brothers.

Often, I hated Ali, my brother, for his freedom, his superiority. One day, I surprised him in the shower. He beat me fiercely so that I could not breathe without pain for a week. His fist drove into my breast.

'I didn't mean to,' I shouted.

'Prying pig.'

'I didn't know.'

He shoved again. At first he had used the flat of his hand, but as he grew more excited he curled his fingers and attacked me with the knuckles. I was fourteen, my breasts were still new, tender. The fist caught me with full force, striking just below my nipple.

'You must never do this again,' he shrieked. 'You will go to hell. You will be a wicked woman. People will stare at you, will wag their fingers. No man will ever marry such a one.'

My amazement at this outburst was only increased by what I had seen. If I had uncovered his nakedness I should have understood; I should have felt that I deserved to be so treated. But the water had not been running down his naked body. Through the steam all I could see was the brown skin of his trunk, and, beneath, the legs and feet. From his navel to his knees, he wore a pair of thin, tight drawers. How could he feel shame that his sister should gaze on him thus? I had always thought that he was not bound as I was, that as a boy he was free. But I see now that he too was shamed by his modesty.

'I shall never marry,' I said. 'I shall never want to.'

As we argued, I struggled against his wet body. He had leaped from the shower like a startled deer from cover, knotted a towel quickly round his thin waist, the clinging drawers just appearing above it. He held my wrists tight in one hand and beat my body with the other.

'You shame us all by this. You must marry, and soon, or it will be too late. You have evil thoughts.'

His voice rose, both in pitch and volume, as we swayed in our anger and strength. I pulled him towards me, to prevent him from being able to swing his arms. Suddenly he stopped, stared at me in fear and rushed out.

'You are bad,' he called. 'You will shame us.'

He was just one year younger than I. His sharp, angular body, hairless and smooth, shook as he held me. The tense, fearful expression as he let me go showed how close he was to disaster. All this seems like a revelation now; then it was a mystery.

But so much was a mystery to us, kept close in our home, never visiting others. Our home, so unlike those on the television programmes and in the stories we read at school.

I did once go to another house, not a friend from school, but a woman my mother knew. They had lived in the same small village in Pakistan when they were girls. Women, now, they lived two streets away from one another in Derby.

The woman's husband had a small shop. It had been a run-down grocer's when they bought it, driven out of business by supermarkets. Now it sold stationery, sweets, groceries, and dried foods, spices, silk off-cuts, and books in Arabic, Urdu, even Italian, for the local Europeans used the shop for their garlic and herbs.

We went to visit when their son was born. I was told it was his naming ceremony, and I wore my best (which meant my nastiest and longest) dress. Ali came unwillingly, hanging back at the last moment, hoping to be left behind in the scramble. He had a secret. We spoke little these days, now that we no longer shared a room. He went to a boy's school, I was at the local Comprehensive for girls. I had passed the examination to go to the Grammar School, but it was mixed, so my father forbade it. He didn't even know that I had taken the exam, at first. This was when my mother would not answer him back. She had agreed with me that many Muslim women were doctors and she hoped that I would be one. But when my father leaned over her and quietly said that I would not go to a school with boys, she just nodded. Later, she found me crying and slapped me.

'You must learn to obey,' she snapped.

'But we agreed. We agreed that it would serve Allah if I became a doctor.'

'You serve Allah by obeying your man, as I do.'

So Ali and I never talked. He did not share his secret as we went to the naming ceremony.

We were the only guests although there were many

people there. The family was large and it honoured the mother's old friend from her village by inviting us. I recognised the Imam, the Prayer-Leader from our own mosque, and although I had never been to afternoon prayers on a Friday, he had visited us.

He greeted us and helped us to find a seat as though he were the host. My mother disappeared quickly into gossip with the other women, leaving Ali and me alone in a large armchair we had to share. The room was very full. I wriggled to get more comfortable and Ali flicked my thigh with the back of his hand.

'Still,' he ordered.

'Nothing's happening,' I hissed.

I wriggled again. 'Give me more room.'

I was beginning to hate Ali. As he grew older, he seemed to think that he could order me around as my father did. I hoped to provoke him into a quarrel which would shame him in company. Wriggling fiercely, I pressed against him.

'More room.'

To my surprise, he flinched away. I had expected a mute and tense wrestling match. As his legs drew away from mine, he reached his hand out and squeezed my thigh, a tight, mean grip which bit into me. At the time I was too angry to be hurt. His body contorted in the strangest way, arm reached out, legs pushed away. This would have developed into an interesting bout if the Imam had not called for silence.

My mother's old friend had come into the room with her baby and her husband. The Imam sat them down in the centre, and turned to the company. He opened a small case and drew out a packet of razor blades. Ali had been still before, but now he was as rigid as death. His hand had been caught on my thigh by the entrance of the family, and when the blades appeared, it hardened its grip. Now I hurt, and I dug my nails into his wrist to force open his hand. At first, he seemed to feel nothing, but slowly his hand opened. All the time his eyes were fixed on the action of the Imam.

When the razor blades were followed by a safety razor Ali looked puzzled. The Imam put the baby into his father's arms and arranged the head pointing towards himself. He screwed a blade into the razor and, with the air of a demonstrator, he pulled it gently with the fall of the hair across the baby's scalp. Looking up at the father, he raised his eyebrows. The father nodded, and the baby was transferred to his mother's arms. Now the Imam watched as the father shaved the baby's head. Ali relaxed for a while, but then he grew uncomfortable again.

The hair was collected and put onto a pair of scales; the equivalent weight given in gold or silver to charity. When all this was completed, the boy's mother announced his name; 'Rashid'. This is one of the ninety-nine names of Allah and means 'guide'.

'Do we eat now?' I asked Ali. But he was still mean and snappy.

'Fool'.

Ready for another attempt at getting him into trouble, I pushed against him in the seat; but I had not noticed my father behind me. He jabbed a knuckle into my back and motioned towards the Imam.

Or, rather, towards where the Imam had been, for now another man stood in his place. I knew this one, too, for he had once opened my blouse and lifted my vest. His fingers had been cold and tickled. I had squirmed against them and my mother had smacked me. Now, he lifted his doctor's bag and rummaged through it. Was the child ill? Perhaps he had come to staunch the flow of blood from the head if the father's hand had slipped. But the shaving had been silent. The fine hair of the baby had yielded to the scrape of blade against skin. He had not put up any resistance or fight.

The doctor mumbled to the mother and gestured to the baby's legs. She removed his nappy and handed him to his father. The little buzz of amused conversation that had followed the weighing of the hair gave way to a strange silence. The doctor held a small pair of clippers, like those my father used to control the hard nail on his toes. I remembered the sharp click they made as the last resistance of the dead cells gave way and the blades met, snapping together. Hair first, now toe nails, I thought. It's like a beauty salon. Ali hissed as he breathed in.

Ignoring the toes completely, the doctor fumbled between Rashid's legs. I twitched with embarrassment. Between his finger and thumb he lifed the little penis. I remembered Ali's and looked at him. It was years since we had bathed together. As I turned to look at him, my eyes went first to the zip on his trousers and then lifted to his eyes. He watched their journey, and his face twisted into something between a smile and a snarl, but he made no noise. His own eyes had only left the action for a second to meet mine, before they returned. The doctor now had the penis in his left hand, the foreskin trapped and stretched between two fingers, while the shaft was in his palm. He looked like a pastry-cook performing a particularly deft piece of manipulation. But instead of popping a confection into the child's mouth, he jabbed forward with the clippers and they clicked shut.

I caught a glimpse of a tiny droplet of blood and would have watched the painting and binding if I could; but as soon as the action was over I heard my father release a lungful of air that he had been holding in and, as I turned to look at him, Ali draped himself lovingly over me, holding me tenderly with one arm, while placing his other hand between my legs.

Before I could wonder how my father and the others would react to this affectionate but unfilial behaviour, I was disabused about its nature. Ali continued to slide, not over me, but down to the floor, leaving a thin trail of vomit over my horrible dress as he went.

The parents were annoyed that Ali had stolen the thunder from their son on the day of his circumcision. My father, I think, that day never accepted Ali as his son; he had shamed him. The other guests were amused, pushing the doctor forward to perform an extra duty to revive him. I understood at last what Ali's secret was. He had known about the ceremony and his adolescent nerves had been too weak. It had only been a nick, I thought. If he had not got himself into such a state he would have been all right. But then, that's what men are like. Even my father had been holding his breath.

Patch's Joy Ride

Usually, if I want something I go out and get it. Not all the time. I mean, I don't just get into parked cars and drive them away if I feel like a ride. Don't laugh. Plenty of people do that. Mickey Singh used to. He was a real prat like that. On the way to school he would walk very close to the curb and quietly lift every car door handle as he passed it. Not obvious, so you could see, and he never stopped talking to do it. You know how when you're little you run a stick along the railings, almost without thinking? Well, that's what it was like with Mickey. And if he found a door open, he'd get in, pull open the bonnet catch, and in two minutes he was off. You didn't see him for the rest of the day.

He never got caught; that was the thing about Mickey. One day he put the car back exactly where it had been parked in the morning and I suppose the guy never knew it had happened, unless he wondered where the petrol had gone. Most times though, he didn't risk putting them back, so he just dumped them when the fuel ran out. Once or twice, when he was beginning and wasn't too good at steering or checking his speed, he took out a bollard or scraped another car, but he would just keep going until he'd put a few streets behind him and then pull up and leave the car. I suppose a few people have had a bit of explaining to do to the police when their numbers have been taken. Can you imagine? Sitting in the office or in a pub and having your car demolish a traffic island? I expect Mickey was lucky they never caught up with him.

We used to walk to school with Mickey a lot, but we didn't often get there together. Mickey was big for fifteen, hard-looking, so people didn't mess with him. He had a second thumb growing out of the side of his real one on his left hand. I couldn't keep my eyes off it when I first knew him.

'Does it work?' I asked. We were only eleven, and it was our first day in the new school. He wasn't any bigger than me then. He only got big later.

'What do you mean?'

'Your thumb. Can you move it?' I pointed at the little joint sticking out from his brown hand.

Mickey didn't answer. He put his face down and ran at me, smashing my nose with the top of his head. I fell, pulling him with me. We scuffled a bit, Mickey punching at me, but not hurting anything like his head had. I lashed out at him and got one or two good ones in. There was quite a lot of blood coming from my nose and by the time the teacher pulled us apart we must have been covered in it. There were the usual questions about who started it, but neither Mickey nor I wanted to answer them, so we both got two strokes of the cane.

'Your first day here,' the Headmaster said. 'I shall be watching you from now on.' And he did. And by the time I was fifteen he had seen a lot more of me. I was getting a bit tired of bending down in front of him and I thought it would have to end soon.

Mickey and I walked quietly away from that first beating. He spoke first. 'No. He said.

'No?'

'No, it doesn't work, I can't move it.'

'That's right,' I said. 'I only wondered.' We got on after that, but I wouldn't get into the cars with him when he started joy-riding. Stands to reason, I think. You'll get caught one day, you always do. But Mickey didn't seem to.

He often asked me to go with him. 'It's great,' he said. 'You can go anywhere you want.'

'No thanks.'

'I'll let you drive.'

But I wasn't bothered about that. I was learning to drive anyway on the old airfield where my dad let me go round in the van. It was great and I wanted to drive a lot. I didn't want to go to court and lose my licence before I got it.

It wasn't just the driving with Mickey, though. He had a car of his own waiting for him to be old enough to start taking proper lessons. His dad got it for his older brothers and they had all learned on it. No, it wasn't the driving. Mickey liked being in a car, closed in, and travelling somewhere.

In lessons, on the days when the local drivers had been sensible enough to lock their doors and Mickey had made it all the way to the school gate without opening one, he would sit in his desk and stare around, fidget with a piece of paper or tap his feet on the floor in time with a song in his head. He just wasn't there.

'Come on, Singh,' the teachers used to say. 'Where are you, lad? You're daydreaming again.'

And Mickey would smile at them, and scratch the side of his nose with the extra thumb that no one ever mentioned, as though it was a death in the family. Mickey was a sort of Sikh. His father was the real thing, but Mickey didn't seem to want to be, but couldn't give it up. He didn't wear a turban or anything, or keep his hair long; in fact, he took a lot of trouble with his hair, having it cut neatly and he was always combing it in the toilets between every lesson, but he always had a silver bracelet, and he carried a little silver dagger with the tip of the handle just sticking out of the top pocket of his blazer.

He was so big and so quick to have a fight that no one ever asked him about it. Except Patch Watkins. Mickey was so taken aback that he didn't think to hit Patch, he just said. 'Oh, you know.'

'No,' said Patch.

Mickey waited a minute, then walked away. I don't think he knew why he did it. But he carried on wearing the bracelet and carrying the dagger.

Patch had a lazy eye. In fact, everything about Patch was lazy. He always missed games, never did any homework and he could tell you exactly what was going on in every series on the television. If they ever have exams on soap operas Patch is going to be a professor. Except, I suppose, that if you had to watch them Patch would give up and start reading. Not that that would be easy. Patch is one of those people who move their lips even when they read silently.

He wore a black patch over his left eye, because the right one was lazy and it had to start working. I know it sounds really good, wearing a black patch, and if someone like Johnnie Sharp or Tony Robbins had to, they'd look terrific. But Patch was pasty-looking and stooped and he had stuck the patch over one side of a cheap pair of specs, so he looked terrible in it. You could always get Patch to do anything. He didn't seem to care or he was too stupid to realise what would happen. Patch really wanted to please people. I suppose he wanted us to like him, but you can't like people like that, can you?

One day we had told Patch that there was going to be a fire drill at half-past ten but that it had to be a surprise to the teachers, so he had to ask to go to the toilet and while he was out of the room he had to push the bell. Well, he did it.

The teachers all went mad because they knew they were always warned about fire drills, so it must be real. I tell you, if that's the way they behave in a panic, we'll all be dead. The Head stormed up and down taking the registers in the yard. Then, when it was all under control he stood facing the whole school. 'I want to know,' he said very slowly, 'who was responsible for pushing the fire bell.' Of course, he knew it was a waste of time asking, but it made him feel better, but as soon as he'd asked the question, Patch stepped forward.

'Stand back, Watkins. Don't get in my way.' He was really working himself up for a shout.

'Sir.' Patch was really keen.

'Shut up!'

'But, Sir.'

'Watkins!'

Patch was getting really upset, he was nearly crying. He still didn't understand what was going on. He had done what they had asked him and he wasn't going to be cheated of his reward. Not in front of the whole school.

'Please, Sir.'

The Head roared this time. 'I must know who pushed the bell.'

Patch's voice rose above him. 'It was me!'

The whole school broke out in cheers and roars of laughter while the Head stared at Patch, proudly looking up at him.

After that Patch managed to fit in better. The six red stripes across his behind were like a row of medals in the changing room and the showers. Patch was sorry when they faded and healed. For a moment he had been a hero.

But we were all surprised when he asked Mickey to take him out in a car. Mickey wasn't very willing. Even the new Patch, the hero, was still only Patch. Mickey didn't want much to do with him. If you hang around with failures you get to be like them.

'You come,' he asked me again. 'You'll like it.' I think Mickey got lonely sometimes, driving around in his cars. I shook my head.

So, Patch and Mickey were both missing one day. And the next day, they were both gone for good.

Mickey had driven the car away, with Patch watching everything he did. Mickey ran the tank fairly low, then pulled in and let Patch get into the driving seat. It was a clear stretch of road and the jerking and jumping as Patch slipped the clutch soon settled down. Patch got into third gear before he heard Mickey shout for him to stop. But he didn't know what he was doing and trod on the accelerator instead of the clutch. He'd never even sat in a driver's seat before.

The car looked terrible afterwards. Crumpled out of shape and twisted like a crippled dog. Mickey was trapped for half an hour while they sawed him out. He only had a few bruises, but all the time he was there Patch's dead face stared round at him, one eye distorted by the smashed glass of the specs, the other hidden by the black tape over the lens.

I still go to school sometimes, but it isn't the same without Mickey. And if I get into trouble, and I do quite a lot, I've made my mind up that they aren't going to cane me any more. I've had enough of that.

I think Mickey could have got away with it. He could have said that Patch had taken the car and that he had only gone along for the ride. But he didn't want to. He told them the truth and then they had him and could check his fingerprints against the files. Then they got angry, but I don't know why. After all, it solved a lot of crimes on their files. Mickey had taken a lot of cars one way and another.

They shouldn't have put him in prison. Not just for taking cars, not even after Patch died. I went to visit him, and he seemed pleased to see me, but he was different. They had taken away his bracelet and his dagger, but he had grown his hair. It was all tied back and fastened with a long cloth. I didn't like to say anything. He couldn't tie a turban properly, but I suppose he'll learn when he gets out. He looked good. Fierce, but kind of in control.

'Don't you mind it here?' I asked.

But he smiled and shook his head. 'It's all right. Those cars. I never wanted them. I just liked sitting inside and riding around.'

He was calm and relaxed, not always tapping and looking around like he had been in school. I don't know. He seemed to have got something. Usually if I want something I go out and get it, but I don't really know what I want yet. But Mickey, he's got something he wants, now, and I want that.

Winter Wind

It had all happened so fast that she could hardly believe that there had been any change in her. In her head she still felt like a young girl; not a child, but certainly not a woman. But her swollen belly, the tired legs that carried her in a swaying, unsteady walk, and the little bumps raising against her skin as the tiny feet and fists revealed the child growing inside her told a different story. She had watched, fascinated, as the child gave up biding its time and began to push and strain to get out. And then it would demand, demand with a far greater intensity than she had so far felt from her family, from her school and from the boy. And how she had buckled beneath the weight of their demands. How, she wondered, would she ever have the strength to answer the child's needs?

It had seemed to begin with the boy, but really the difficulties started long before that. Fatima liked school too much. She tried to stay behind after lessons, to join clubs, to help with plays, to sing in the choir. Always there seemed to be a reason why she could not.

'It is not right for so young a girl to be out at night,' her father insisted while her mother sat, close-lipped and secret.

'But you want me to be good at school,' Fatima argued,

too young to know the value of silence, the power of submission.

'You can be good in lessons. There is no need for these games.'

'Games,' Fatima shouted, proving her unworthiness to her father. 'These are not games. We learn through them. I want to help at school and the teacher admires my singing.'

'Singing,' her father snatched the word in triumph. 'You want to sing hymns and songs to their God. You want to leave us. Well, you can't. You belong to us, not to them.'

Fatima recognised the disaster that faced her and made no reply, but her clenched fists were more true to her feelings than her tight lips.

'And plays. What is this plays? What do you want with such things? It is not modest.'

This was too much for her. It was unjust. 'I was not to be in a play. I only wanted to help backstage.' She should not have used the unfamiliar word.

'Helping is as bad. Not modest is not modest. Whether it is you, or whether you help another.'

And so the gap grew, and the boy slipped into it, filling the space between Fatima and her family. Her mother always kept mute in these struggles, a critical, but undeclared audience.

The victor in a great struggle often allows small concessions to the vanquished. After several punishing rows, Mr Ali sensed the distance that was growing between him and the daughter he loved. He was also getting tired of the fierce opposition of his wife. In front of their daughter, Mrs Ali was completely loyal to her husband. She never spoke against him. It would be a bad example, and the girl was bad enough already, nearly as bad as those English girls who had no respect for their fathers or their husbands. But in private, in the soft darkness of their room, Mrs Ali broke out from her passive attitude of a spectator and assumed the principal role.

'We must understand her,' she urged her husband. 'She will do things without telling us if we do not let her share with her friends.'

'She should do as she is told,' he would argue.

'But we will lose her.' Mrs Ali could be persuasive as well as strong.

'We cannot lose. She is ours,' Mr Ali struggled.

'Perhaps we need to be careful if we want her.'

Mr Ali lay back unhappily and agreed. So when the note came from the school about the trip to the theatre, he was prepared. His wife's glare checked his automatic objection and he paused, thoughtfully. Fatima had been sullen and disappointed until she saw his considered hesitation.

'This is work,' he said impressively. His pen hovered over the paper. 'Your teacher says you must see this play,' he stumbled a little over the word as though it were a piece of bad food that lodged in his mouth, 'because it is for your examination.'

'It is. It is,' Fatima agreed. 'I don't think I will ever understand it if I do not see it.' She smiled at him. 'I learn it by heart, but I do not understand it yet.'

The pen scratched the paper. It was signed. Mrs Ali smiled with happiness and relief. They spent a happy evening.

Fatima's excitement grew as the date of the theatre visit drew closer. She was more careful than usual not to upset her father, ready to accept his opinions and orders rather than risk a sudden change of heart. There were signs that he might withdraw permission as the days went on. He was troubled that he had given in. Was it right for her to go? Did he spoil her by allowing it? But fear of his wife's anger combined with a genuine desire to let his daughter have something that seemed right and the visit went ahead.

For Fatima it was as exciting as a journey to another world. The hum of conversation in the foyer, the programmes, the faded blue seats, the stage laid out with costumes that the characters assumed as they arrived to take their places in the drama; all the artifice of planner and playwright captivated her.

As the actors went through the monotony of their parts Fatima mouthed the words with them. She learned quickly and knew many of the speeches and all of the songs.

When the house lights went up for the interval she turned to the seat next to her and grabbed the arm of the boy. 'It is wonderful,' she said.

Colin was taken aback. He too enjoyed the play, but it did not move him as it did her. He sat next to her because he had no friends in the class. Fatima could not be called a friend, but she was polite to him and he could talk to her sometimes. In schools there are always boys, awkward and uncoordinated, who feel themselves to be no better than the others, who would like to play in teams and hang around in groups in the evenings, but who are never asked. They lack both prowess and the personality needed to make a success in the adolescent world. Colin was one of these. His relationship with Fatima had come about because of his isolation from the rest of the class, but to some extent it also made things worse. So he was startled when she grabbed his arm, but a little pleased.

'Yes,' he agreed, but didn't know where to go from there.

But Fatima didn't need any help. She launched into a description of what they had just seen and the way it made the play different for her. The forest, the wrestling bout, the hunt, the exiled lords living under the greenwood, had been strange distant figures and scenes only an hour ago, but now they were a real world.

Colin listened, and the play became for him, too, alive and important. As Fatima spoke to him, she too took on a new meaning for him. He was disappointed when the auditorium darkened again and the cast took the stage.

Fatima's father was glad he had let her go to theatre when she got home that night. Often, recently, she had been difficult and unhappy, but now her eyes and lips matched one another when she smiled. He had not seen such unmixed and obvious joy since she was a tiny child, thrilled with a new sound or toy, or just the fact of his presence after a brief absence. He held her tight to him as she thanked him for giving his permission. At the other side of the room her mother watched the two with simple pleasure.

In her desk at school the next day Fatima found a card. It was a postcard from the theatre, showing the stylised trees of the Forest of Arden overshadowing Rosalind and Orlando. On the back was written:

Under the Greenwood tree
Who loves to lie with me,
And turn his merry note
Unto the sweet bird's throat,
Come hither, come hither, come hither.
Here shall he see
No enemy
But winter and rough weather.

Colin was nowhere in sight.

It was not easy for them to meet. Fatima was not allowed far from home without reason and it was unthinkable that Colin could visit her at home. But the success of the theatre visit made her father more tolerant of school activities. The choir remained forbidden because of the Christian music, but helping at the play was allowed and so were some clubs as long as they did not involve sport, which would not be modest. Colin discovered an interest in lighting which he had not suspected before and the jerky fashion of amateur rehearsal left ancilliary workers like them plenty of time to spend in conversation.

There was one day when Colin heard a conversation in which his name was mentioned and a laugh went up, then the word 'wogs' and a further laugh, and Colin wished he was more athletic. But on the whole his previous experience of isolation had been so bad that he was grateful for Fatima and willing to impose a diplomatic deafness when it was necessary.

Freedom from school during the examinations gave them more time together and Colin's house, empty during the day, gave them somewhere to meet. So, long before the results of the exams fell through the door, Fatima's mother noticed her daughter's sickness in the mornings.

Mr Ali's anger was the most frightening thing Fatima had ever seen. Her mother too was angry, but there was a protective coating over her reaction. She tried to help. 'She is still our daughter, whatever happens. She is a good girl.'

'A good girl.' Mr Ali did not know how to answer such a lie. 'Does a good girl do such a thing?'

Fatima shook, as much with fear for what she had done as for dread of the anger of the man.

'Who has done this?' was the repeated demand. But Fatima would give no answer.

Violent words gave way to blows and both Fatima and her mother were shaken and hurt when Mr Ali finally left the two women alone.

'You ask her. You find out what is this. What this truth is that cannot be said.'

But kindness was no more effective than rage and Fatima hugged her secret to her, its importance growing as the baby inside her did.

Where Fatima had been sullen, now her father was. He grew a garment of darkness over their lives.

'She is no daughter of mine,' he would insist when his wife talked about her.

At last Fatima made the decision to spare her mother any more trouble and left. So when the baby threw her into contractions, Fatima was alone, under the care of a charity.

She lay, in a world that was no world. No light from outside could enter the gloom of the dimly-lit delivery-room. No sound but the humming of the lights and the machines checking pulse-rate and heart-beat. The midwife, in the sterile white of the overalls, leaned over her and whispered.

'Nearly there, now. Will you give me another big push?'

Fatima clenched her jaw and nodded.

When she finally sank back, with her own daughter in her tired arms, hands exhausted from gripping, Fatima looked around the empty room. In the antiseptic void of this hospital she held her child. She remembered her father disowning her. Lifting the tiny body to her, she breathed softly into her right ear the Adhan, the words that every new Muslim first hears on this earth.

God is the greatest.
I bear witness that there is no other god but Allah.
I bear witness that Muhammad is the messenger of Allah.
Come to prayer.
Come to security.

God is the greatest.
There is no God but Allah.

The ceremony half-done, she turned the child and drew her lips to her left ear. A smile passed across them before she murmured:

Who doth ambition shun,
And loves to live i' th' sun,
Seeking the food he eats,
And pleased with what he gets,
Come hither, come hither, come hither,
Here shall he see
No enemy
But winter and rough weather.

Taking Care

The little house had always been noisy; uncles and aunts, cousins and friends had treated it as home. Children were always scrambling over the worn furniture, stamping in the narrow passageway, or squealing echoes in the alley down the side. There were parties for every occasion. If a new baby was born they all came here. When marriages were due, the grown-ups sat around this tiled fireplace and planned. And always, Umar sat in his great chair, grey streaks of hair running from his temples through to his beard. No decision was made without his approval; every new baby was ceremoniously presented to him, cradled in his strong arms, and gently rested on his huge lap; he gave generously both to the newly-married and the poor. Umar was the engine that drove the powerful, intricate machine that was Aisha's family. Umar provided the strength, the money and the reason for everything. For Aisha, he was more than just a father, he was life and meaning.

'Ask your father,' her mother would say. And Aisha would come up behind his throne, place her hand on his shoulder and wait. Umar always knew it was her, wondered sometimes why she chose to stand behind him when she had something to ask, a favour or request.

'Aisha. Sit down.' She would come around the chair.

Even now, sixteen, she would lower herself onto his lap, arm around his neck. He loved her to whisper to him, to ask his permission the way she had as a toddler, when his bulk, though less then, had still seemed to her the most massive human expression of power and protection.

A child of his old age, Aisha stood alone in Umar's affections and regard. There was little he did not grant her. Only once could she remember his anger to her. Two new members of the family had arrived from the old country. The house had not been still for four days as they told their stories, brought news of those left behind, were given new clothes for the winter they had made no plans for. They were fed and introduced, they were honoured guests until a home of their own could be arranged. Aisha, only ten, turned to her father on the third day.

'When will we have the house for ourselves, again?' she asked.

Umar's face set hard. He hauled himself from his great chair without a word and took her arm. She squealed as the fingers dug into her. In silence he half-dragged, half-carried her up to her room. Aisha feared a beating, although her father had never once struck her; all smacks had come from the hands of her mother. But there was no slap, no chastisement. With frightening control and quietness he spoke to her.

'And so,' he finished, 'you will say sorry. You will say that this house is their house for as long as they honour us by staying here. And please, you will never again insult our friends with your selfishness. One day, you will know the story of the goodness we have had from others, and you will be ashamed.'

'But you do not talk,' she complained.

'What is this?'

But she had said all she knew how. She put her arms

around the front of his stomach and clung to him. 'I am sorry,' she said.

'It is done. No more. We will go downstairs, and I will talk until your ears ache.'

There were tears of shame in Aisha's eyes as she apologised. The guests were gracious, but they knew it was time for them to go. They could not meet Umar's eyes, but turned to look at the frost-flowers sketched on the window panes. They had never seen ice or snow before, and every year afterwards, with the first frost of winter they remembered the days spent in Umar's house, and his strange, resentful little girl. For her part, Aisha never saw a window decorated with the frost without shivering, not for cold, but for shame.

As time passed Aisha learned to share her father with the many close friends and distant relatives who met in their house. When they were not there he was hers. Her hand on his shoulder: 'Aisha'. And she would slide round to sit on his knee.

Then, one day, the chair was empty when she came home from school. For a week Umar lay in bed. Every day Aisha would sit for an hour, strictly limited by the doctor. She told him about her day at school, about what the news had said on the television, about her plans to go on to college, to learn shorthand and typing. He lay and listened, her hand gently but firmly held in his. His breath came quickly, with a strange grinding that sounded painful to Aisha, but which seemed not to trouble him.

In the evenings Aisha would look at his chair. Once, she moved across and sat down in it. She stared around, expecting the room to look different from there, perspectives lengthened, shadows lightened, she felt as though she should be able to see more clearly, feel more acutely, as though the chair itself would confer on her the power and authority of the old man. But nothing was different, except that without the cushion of his large frame the chair was knobbly and hard, unwelcoming and discomforting. She went to bed.

On the sixth day after he took to his bed she sat next to him. He put a document in her hand. 'Read.'

Her name seemed to appear a lot of times throughout the text, as though she had become important.

For the first time ever, she lied to her father. 'I do not understand,' she said.

He did not answer, but looked at her, and she was accused.

The door opened. 'You must leave now.' Her mother was ruthless in enforcing the doctor's instructions. Aisha stood and laid the document on the bed. The strong old hand lifted it to her.

'Take it.'

'Time to go.'

Aisha looked from father to mother. The woman's eyes were expressionless. The document hovered.

Slowly, Aisha took the stiff legal paper. She hung her head and left the room. Her mother lingered, a small smile growing on her lips as she contemplated her husband's closed eyes and crumpled face.

It was a whole day before the girl could talk to her father about the contract.

'Why?'

'You must be looked after,' he said.

His voice was different. The trembling, and the breathlessness, these were not like him. Aisha hoped it was emotion that made it so, but knew it was not, knew that he struggled for every word. The room was hot and stuffy; outside the air was still and close, and there was no breath of breeze, no movement; the sun beat down.

It was as though his tired chest could not suck in the heavy air.

'We can manage.' Aisha was frightened to argue, but determined to insist. She winced at the pain the old man needed to fill his lungs.

'It is someone else's turn.' The words came slowly, from muddy depths.

'No.'

'I have arranged.'

Aisha hated herself for the pain she was inflicting. 'I can make other arrangements. I shall look after you, until you are better.'

Her mother's voice broke in. Aisha had been concentrating so fiercely that she had not heard the door open. 'Go, child.'

'It is not time,' Aisha protested.

'You tire him. You argue. It is not good. Only when you please him can you stay the whole time.' The voice was even but strong.

Aisha picked up her father's hand. Kissed it. He smiled at her.

'Tomorrow.'

She nodded.

At school the next day she stared at the other girls. She had thought that she was like them. She asked herself how this could be, but no answer came. She could find no reason, but there was still a choice to make.

Extraordinarily, the house still quivered with the beat of childish feet and the growling of adult conference. Aisha longed for silence in the rooms, but the momentous event taking place in her father's bedroom sent waves of magnetism through the neighbourhood, drawing people in to discuss and confer, to murmur early condolences and words of comfort, to repay old hospitality and new debts.

Aisha looked at some, older men, who contemplated her father's position with greedy faces. She sat, away from the rumbling activity, holding his hand.

'I have decided.'

He listened.

'It is not what I want.' She looked carefully at his face as she told her story. His eyes did not shut, he made no attempt to speak. For many minutes she spoke of what she had longed for. When she finished, there was a long pause. He tempted her to go on. She sat.

'You have not,' he said, painfully, 'given me an answer.'

'I know.'

'Well?'

'It is not what I want.' The same non-committal disclaimer.

'Next week, perhaps tomorrow, what you want will not matter. Someone will decide for you. I would rather it should be me.' The long speech cost him a lot.

'Yes,' she agreed. 'It should be you.'

'He is a good man.'

'Of course.' She stroked his hand. 'I will marry this man,' she promised. 'For you.'

The next day she sat again at his bedside, this time with another. The man was ten years older than her; his broad face could not compose itself into an expression. Sorrow and pride fought on equal terms to gain possession of his features. The old man nearly failed to complete the blessing, but his breath did not disgrace him. The young man was gentle in his farewell and compassionate in his decision to leave father and daughter together rather than take her from the room with him.

'Thank you, father.'

'You are dutiful. He is a good man.'

The care of the old man's body was the duty of the men.

The rites were celebrated, the prayers recited. Aisha wished she could be involved, but it was not seemly.

On the day of the funeral she stood under a tree in the cemetary. The shade was gentle after the cruel heat on the dry pavement. She was hidden from the little knot of mourners and could only dimly make out what was happening. She could hear nothing. A broken angel stretched out its arms above her, one wing snapped, the nose and eyes smudged by wind and rain into a sightless mask. All the graves around her ran east-west, so that the dead could spring up on the last day facing the rising sun. But her father's body was being laid at an angle to these, in a special section, where the Sons of the Prophet would face Mecca. Aisha stood, in a green shade, watched blindly by her angel, pointing the wrong way. In her hand she carried a small bag with a change of clothes, some shoes and her toothbrush.

She squinted at the men. They obscured her father's grave, but something about the stoop of their shoulders told her when he was lowered in.

'Goodbye,' she whispered, and clutched the handle of her bag. 'And I'm sorry, but I must decide for myself.'

When the group broke up she pressed against the tree. They were not passing her, but she feared discovery. She watched them as far as the gate and through the railings. As they left, one hung back. He returned along the gravel path to the new grave. She recognised the solid, chubby body and broad face of the man her father had chosen as her husband. He stood over the mound of soft earth.

He looked up as she drew near. 'I thought you would be here.'

'But I am not allowed.'

'Yes, I know that. I think perhaps that is really why you are here.'

Aisha stood, avoiding contact. 'We had better go,' she said.

'He was a good man.'

Aisha looked fiercely at him. 'That is what he said about you.'

'Only you can decide that,' he said.

'Yes. I must decide. He was wrong to force me, perhaps. But I do not think he would mind that I insist on making up my own mind.'

He nodded.

She held out her bag for him to take.

'We had better go,' she repeated.